For Molly
Enjoy!

Joy

CeeGee's Gift

a novel

Joy H. Selak

Published by JoyWrites
Austin, TX
joywrites.com

Cover design by Jennifer Braham
Interior Design by Danielle H. Acee
Editing by Dan Selak, Cathy Casey, and Danielle H. Acee

ISBN: 9781-7322831-1-4 Hardcover
Cataloging-in Publication Data
Selak, Joy
CeeGee's Gift/Joy H. Selak
Library of Congress Control Number: 2018906598

First printing edition 2019.

For my mother Charlotte Ann Agee Hubbard

She awakened each day to a brand-new world,
and took me along on her journey of discovery.

And for my Auntie Leone Hubbard Jackson

Like every child who knew her,
I was sure I was her favorite.

The Great Tide Pool…is a fabulous place:
when the tide is in, a wave churned basin,
creamy with foam, whipped by the combers
that roll in from the whistling buoy on the reef.
But when the tide goes out
the little water world becomes quiet and lovely.

The smells of life and richness, of death and digestion,
of decay and birth, burden the air.
And salt spray blows in from the barrier where the ocean waits
for its rising tide strength to permit it back into the Great Tide Pool again.

John Steinbeck, *Cannery Row,* 1945

Chapter One

Mr. Tindale lived in an old wooden one-story house with three broad steps up to a wide covered porch. The newer houses on Magdalena Island, especially the ones close to the beach, were built up high on stilts and people parked their cars in the shady spaces underneath. That way when the hurricanes roared in from the Gulf of Mexico and flood tides washed over the island, only people's cars would drown, instead of whole houses and families. Everyone in town figured the Tindales must have Divine Storm Protection because no matter how hard the storms hit, their house always stayed high and dry—even without the stilts.

CeeGee arrived on Friday after school let out and found Mr. Tindale sitting in his front porch rocker, as usual, with Mrs. Tindale's rocker looking sad and empty beside him. Spunk the cat was asleep on top of the porch rail. CeeGee left her bike at the end of the drive, opened the mailbox on top of the post and took out the mail. Then she crossed the sand-spattered yard and climbed the steps, "So, how are you this afternoon, Mr. Tindale?" she asked as she handed him the mail.

"I'm all right," he said, taking the envelopes. "You know, Celia Gene, it's not so easy for me to get down those steps, what with my bad leg and all, so it's kind of you to bring up my mail. How 'bout you, missy?"

"I'm okay," CeeGee pushed her glasses up on her nose and got right to it. "Listen, I was wondering, you need some help with your garden here?" She pointed at the bed below the porch, a tangle of dry, top-heavy perennials scattered among a variety of weeds.

"What?" He glanced down, "You sayin' my garden's a mess?"

"Well, yes sir. Besides, I have to do fifteen hours of community service for seventh grade and my mom says you might be the person I should help."

"How long you got?"

"Till the end of school."

"That ain't long, is it?"

"No, sir, I only have two weeks left."

He shook his head and gave her a once-over. "Hmmm, in that case, you better get to work." He looked down at the flower bed. "Now that I'm looking at it, this garden is a mess."

"That's just what I was thinking." CeeGee grinned up at him. "Is it okay if I start tomorrow morning?"

"Saturday, that will be just fine. All right, I'll be waitin' for ya."

CeeGee rode her bike six blocks to the Southport Public Library, which was on the same street as the Magdalena Island Public Schools—elementary, junior high and high school—all in a row with the ball fields in the open space behind them. She parked her bike in the rack, pulled open the big wooden door and went straight to the main desk. Miss McGuire ignored her, as usual, so CeeGee busied herself looking through the returned book cart. The librarian did some filing, straightened a few stacks of papers and fussed with her hair.

"Your hair looks real nice today, Miss McGuire," CeeGee finally said to end the standoff.

Miss McGuire looked up, eyes wide with fake surprise, and patted at her hair. "Why, thank you, Celia Gene, I do try to keep myself looking nice."

"In case your Knight in Shining Armor comes, right?"

"Precisely. One never knows when one's knight might appear. Why, he might come right through that door at any moment," Miss McGuire got a moony look on her face and stared at the front entrance, "and sweep me off my feet." She turned back to CeeGee, "And then I will live happily ever after."

"That would be real nice, Miss McGuire."

"I do try to keep myself ready—every moment, for that perfect man to come into my life." She brushed at some imaginary lint on her skirt. "It's not an easy task, let me tell you, not an easy task whatsoever."

CeeGee had been listening to Miss McGuire talk about her knight for as far back as she could remember, long enough to figure out all this waiting and primping and staring across the room made no sense at all. CeeGee even read some books about knights to see if there could be any truth to Miss McGuire's story, but it didn't take a child genius to figure out there were no knights in shining armor, not in this day and age. And even if there were, one wasn't likely to come busting into the Southport Public Library on a white horse, so he could sweep Miss McGuire off her feet and gallop away to live happily ever after. CeeGee thought Miss McGuire spent way too much time with her nose stuck in old-timey books.

"Celia Gene, how are you coming with my list?"

"I quit reading from the list since you wouldn't let me check out *The Great Gatsby*, Miss McGuire."

"I told you child, F. Scott Fitzgerald is not an appropriate author for your age group. I did not compile 'Miss McGuire's Personal List of the Best Books by American Authors' specifically for twelve-year-old children."

"I'm nearly thirteen."

"Nearly thirteen then, Celia Gene." Miss McGuire raised her hand and swept the air as if to reveal a banner floating in the sky and recited, "I am just doing my duty to protect island youth from nefarious literature."

CeeGee knew what nefarious meant because she had looked it up in the library's big dictionary the first time Miss McGuire said it. It meant 'evil' and 'wicked' and naturally made CeeGee want to read all the books Miss McGuire wouldn't let her check out, especially *The Great Gatsby*. "Miss McGuire, my dad says if I am able to read a book, I should be allowed to read the book. And besides, like I said, I'm nearly thirteen, and my dad says I'm old enough to read whatever I want."

Miss McGuire harrumphed before she replied, "Your father is not the head librarian of the Southport Public Library, now is he? I do not tell him how to run his pharmacy, so he can just keep his nose out of my library business. There is much going on in *The Great Gatsby* that you do not yet need to know about, young lady. I will allow you to check it out when you are sufficiently mature."

CeeGee decided not to tell Miss McGuire her dad also said he had half a mind to go down to the library and give the old bat a piece of his mind. Or that her mom invited her to skip ahead to the S's on Miss McGuire's list and read John Steinbeck's *Cannery Row* along with the sophomore English class she taught at the high school. CeeGee knew Miss McGuire wouldn't approve of reading books out of order, or all the parties and drinking that went on in *Cannery Row*. "I'm here for books on gardening today," CeeGee said. "I'm going to be a volunteer gardener."

Miss McGuire also harrumphed at that, as if she didn't approve of CeeGee reading any books that weren't on her list, but she grudgingly took her over to the gardening section. CeeGee leafed through every single book on the shelves. One was about zone gardening. She looked at the map in the front of the book where it showed all the zones for the whole United States. CeeGee knew that Magdalena Island, Texas, was on the Texas

Coastal Bend. It was easy to find the bend on the map. It was the long arc of coastline that stretched from the southern tip of Texas all the way to the Louisiana border, but tiny Magdalena Island was just a dot near the middle and her town of Southport wasn't on the map at all. Still, CeeGee could tell Magdalena was in Zone 9, so she figured she'd only have to read that one part of the book. Another book was called *Flowering Plants of Texas*. CeeGee hoped this one might help her recognize the most important plants, so she wouldn't yank something special out of Mr. Tindale's garden thinking it was just a weed. CeeGee took the books to the checkout counter.

"So," Miss McGuire asked, "what, may I ask, has brought on this interest in gardening, Celia Gene?"

"I have to do a community service project before school lets out and my mom thought helping Mr. Tindale with his flower bed might be good."

"And how is that kind old man?"

"He seems a little sad to me. A little lonely."

"That is not surprising, not in the slightest. He and his dear wife, Maggie May, were two peas in a pod, that they were. It must be hard on him, all alone, now that she has passed."

"Spunk helps some, but I'm hoping maybe I can help out too, at least that's what my mom thinks."

"Well, I do understand, Celia Gene," Miss McGuire reached out and patted CeeGee's hand. "The Tindales, while having no offspring of their own, always took care to be kind to children, so it's only fitting that you offer some kindness to him in return on these sorrowful days. In spite of your rebellious spirit about adhering to my list, Celia Gene, you do have a kind and generous heart."

"Gee, thanks for saying that." Celia looked down at her feet for a moment while she flushed pink among her freckles, then looked up and added, "You remember how the Tindales always sat on the porch and waved to all the kids when we rode by on our bicycles? They liked it when we stopped and talked to them. And they had the best Halloween treats—and they never got mad, even when we kicked a ball into the flower bed."

"Exactly right, that was the two of them in a nutshell. Together, smiling and waving, accepting of children, who I might add, aren't always so easy to tolerate. Well then, child, you best be on your way, so you can study up and make Maggie May's old flower bed shiny bright." She stamped the books and handed them to CeeGee. "But don't forget my list, as soon as possible, you must get back to your serious reading."

"Yes, ma'am." CeeGee took both books from the library, loaded them into her bicycle basket, rode home and read them through before dinner.

The next morning, CeeGee put on her work clothes and rode her bike back over to Mr. Tindale's. He took her to the garage behind the house, pulled open the big double doors and helped her find Mrs. Tindale's old garden tools stuck in a bucket of sand. This made him so sad he had to go indoors for a while, but he soon came back out to the porch with two glasses of sweet tea. He put one on the wicker table beside his rocker and one on the porch rail, then sat down to watch as CeeGee began to weed, prune, stake and water. Every once in a while, CeeGee would reach up to take a sip of tea. Pretty soon they were chatting like old friends. After that weekend, CeeGee brought Mr. Tindale's mail to him every day on her way home from school and stayed on an hour or so to do a little work and visit. After she finished her gardening, she'd hose off the tools, stick them in the bucket of sand and go sit on the top porch step. Spunk would rub against her leg while Mr. Tindale used his special pocket knife to peel them an apple in one long spiral. He'd cut the apple into sections and pass one over to her, eat the next one himself, give one to her—back and forth until the apple was gone. Sometimes they'd eat two apples.

While he was peeling and eating, he'd talk about what he read in the newspaper that morning and ask CeeGee what she learned at school that day. He asked her about her friends and her teachers and all that she was learning. CeeGee didn't have much to say about friends, because she really didn't have any, but she told him all the rest. In no time at all the colorful perennials—purple sage and hyssop, rusty orange butterfly weed and all the pinks of the phlox—began to perk up on their stalks. Their blossomed heads tilted toward the porch as if listening to what the two were saying.

One of the things Mr. Tindale liked to talk about most, naturally, was his dear wife Maggie May, silver-haired, but still spry and full of life when she suddenly up and died a few months before. Mr. Tindale told CeeGee that for a while after Maggie died, he could still feel her with him, right there by his side. He said they wandered around the house and yard together, sharing their memories. In time, Maggie May paled and moved on. Mr. Tindale said he had no idea where the dead went, but he was sure it was more interesting than hanging around with him doing nothing, so he didn't blame her for leaving. Still, the loss changed him. "There's no good reason for me to be here on this earth with my dear, dear Maggie May gone from it," he said, shaking his head.

It didn't come as any surprise to CeeGee that Mr. Tindale spent some time with his wife even after she passed on. When CeeGee was little, she could see a light shimmering around Mr. Tindale's head, like a rainbow. She tried to tell her parents about it, "Momma, Daddy, look! Pretty colors!" But they couldn't see Mr. Tindale's light, any more than they could see CeeGee's own light when it came down from above and entered her. CeeGee wondered if Mr. Tindale's light had brought him nothing but trouble like hers had, and if he snuffed it out the same way she did. Then she thought that maybe his light was still there, but she just couldn't see it anymore. Or maybe, when Maggie May left this earth, Mr. Tindale was just too sad to have that rainbow around his head. She didn't ask him any questions about his light though, because the last thing in this world she wanted was to talk about hers. She'd managed to keep her light from coming for three years, and she wasn't going to ruin everything now.

✫ ✫ ✫ ✫

One day, Mr. Tindale brought their tea out to the porch, like usual, and looked down over the rail at CeeGee hard at work in the flowerbed. He eased himself into his rocker, propped his cane against the railing and began to brood. "You know," he finally said, "I always figured I was pretty good at doing stuff, but since Maggie's gone I'm all thumbs. I can't iron worth a fiddle, so now I just put on old wrinkled shirts. I must look a sight. My Maggie would roll over in her grave, she would." The rocker treads whacked louder and louder as he pushed back and forth. "And I'm no good at all in the kitchen. Yesterday when I took a glass out of the dishwater it slipped out of my hand and broke. Then, when I reached in after it, I cut my thumb." He held up his right hand for CeeGee to see the bandage. "Now I only got one thumb left to be clumsy with." He took a drink of his tea and banged the glass back down on the wicker table. "And laundry! Maggie May used to fold up those fitted bed sheets so's they sat on the shelf in neat little squares, straight as you please. Can you do that? I can't do that to save my life."

CeeGee got up from where she'd been weeding the bed, brushed the dirt off her knees and glanced skyward. She swatted at a brief flash of light. "None of that stuff matters, Mr. Tindale," she announced.

"Course it matters. These are everyday chores, have to be done."

"What I mean is…" she paused a moment as the beam from above pulsed into her, then said in a rush, "What I mean is, if you have something you need to do, well, you'd best do it—and soon."

"What in heaven's name are you rambling on about, child?" He looked impatient.

"I just have a feeling…"

"If you have something to say, speak up." Mr. Tindale leaned forward, put his hands on his knees and waited.

CeeGee wiped her forehead with the back of her hand and pushed her glasses up on her nose. "Fact is you don't have much time, Mr. Tindale. So, you best get yourself ready. Your time is real short."

"What would you know about my time?"

"I know you don't have much."

"Of course, I don't have much, I'm an old man! And you can just keep your facts and feelings to yourself, young lady, because I ain't leaving this here earth until I'm good and ready." Mr. Tindale had been telling CeeGee for days on end that he wanted nothing more than to join Maggie May wherever she was, but now that his wish was about to come true, he'd have none of it. "And who do you think you are anyway, some kind of soothsayer?"

"What's a soothsayer?"

"Some fool who thinks he can tell the future."

"Well then, I'm a soothsayer, sure enough."

"Hogwash. You ain't no such thing." He used his cane to push himself out of the rocker and glared down at her.

He was getting red in the face and CeeGee was afraid if he got too mad he'd keel over right in front of her. "I… I'm sorry, Mr. Tindale, maybe I'd better just hush up and get on home."

"Maybe you better." He turned and started for the door, muttering, "My time is short, what kind of foolish talk is that?"

CeeGee left without another word, her dirt-caked tools scattered all over the flowerbed. Behind her, she could hear the angry rap, rap, rap of Mr. Tindale's cane as he walked across the wooden porch. She heard him yank open his creaky screen door and heard it slam it shut behind him. Then she was alone in the terrible silence. CeeGee knew what just happened was all her fault. She'd let the light come in and told a Knowing. Now another person in Southport, someone she truly cared for, was bound to die.

Chapter Two

The first week of summer should be the best time of all, but for CeeGee it was an agony of waiting. Every day, CeeGee went straight to her dad's drugstore and grabbed a newspaper off the rack to see if there was any news of Mr. Tindale. There wasn't. Then she went home and positioned herself by the front window in the living room, so she could see both the street and the kitchen where the phone hung on the wall above the counter. She listened for sirens and eavesdropped when her mother was talking on the phone. Any day now, she knew, the news would come. But after a whole week—nothing.

On Saturday morning, CeeGee sat at the kitchen table, checking to see if Mr. Tindale's obituary was in the weekend paper that got delivered to their house. Bobbie turned from the stove where she was making a late breakfast, pointed at her daughter with the spatula and said, "Celia Gene, what in heaven's name is the matter with you?"

CeeGee looked up, startled, and quickly closed the paper. "Why nothin', Momma."

"It is the first week of summer and you are sitting here at home. You're making me nervous. I want you to get on outside today and get some fresh air, you hear?" She turned to the stove and flipped the eggs, "Thirteen years old and sitting around the house reading the paper. I never."

"I'm not thirteen till next week, Momma."

Bobbie turned back to her daughter, "I know that, Celia Gene. But when you are thirteen you will still be too young to spend a beautiful day sitting indoors reading the paper. You're turning into your father. Why don't you go over and visit Mr. Tindale? He'd probably like some company. You can go to the Triple S and get some ice cream, or go to the beach, or the marsh. Just get out and do something."

"Yes, ma'am."

After breakfast, CeeGee got dressed in shorts and a sleeveless cotton shirt and put on the sneakers she wore for bike riding. She felt nervous about leaving, in case the news finally came, but she knew she'd feel even worse if she disobeyed her mother. Bobbie Williamson was feisty and strong, and taught English at the high school. She was petite, with tiny hands and perfect pale skin, but she also had hair the color of a polished copper penny, pinned up on top of her head like a shining crown. CeeGee always figured it was the hair that gave her mother her power. That, and being whip smart, like English teachers ought to be. Everyone, including CeeGee, took care not to get into trouble with Bobbie Williamson.

CeeGee had red hair too, but it definitely did not make her feel feisty and strong, just awkward and different. It was a thick, dull, rust-colored mop and CeeGee thought it made her look like an oversized doll wearing an old, worn-out wig. In addition to the hair, CeeGee was extra tall like her dad, taller than any boy in her whole junior high school, with skinny long legs and a full constellation of freckles scattered across her nose. Plus, she wore glasses. People said she was smart, but she wasn't so sure that was true because only grownups said it, not kids. Her big brothers, Danny and Davey, had special names for her like Four Eyes and Bird Legs and Stick Doll, which didn't help. Plus, they were twins which made it easier for them to gang up.

CeeGee said goodbye to her mother in the kitchen, who gave her that look, a combination of tough and soft, as only she could do. CeeGee went down the stairs to the carport and got her bike, pedaled two blocks down to the end of Seaward Street, took a left on Beach, rode another three blocks to the top of Beacon and took a right. About three thousand people lived in Southport year-round and Beacon Street, five blocks long, was what they called Town. Beacon was mostly a street of ones: one grocery store, one liquor store, one movie theater, one bank, one bakery and, right in the middle, the one drugstore and soda shop that her dad owned. Southport hadn't changed in forever—the people, the town, even the stores. It was like it was set in the pages of a book written long ago and everybody was fine with the story that it told—especially all the tourists who came every summer.

Southport was on the southeast end of Magdalena Island and separated from the mainland by a narrow shipping channel. People came and left the island either on the two ferries that crossed the channel every five minutes to the mainland, or drove over one long causeway on the western side. In summer, tourists poured off the ferries to visit the island's beaches and, because of them, some things in Southport came in dozens—like beach cottages, bars and fish houses, boat and bicycle rentals and especially souvenir shops, which the locals called Tacky Stores.

Once inside a tacky store it was easy to see how they got the nickname, as every single one had rows and rows of cheap products for sale, most of them made of shells. There were shell necklaces and bracelets, shell-covered boxes, shell wind chimes hanging from the ceiling, and bins filled with all different kinds of shells, each with a handwritten label stuck on the front. The tacky stores also had rows of items with *Southport, Texas,* or *Magdalena Island* printed on them, some with a map of Texas and a big star at the bottom for Southport. There were hanging racks of T-shirts and beach cover-ups, and shelves of beach towels. There were refrigerator magnets, key chains, ashtrays, shot glasses, placemats and glass globes with sand in them, all heralding this tiny dot in the great, big Lone Star State.

On top of that the tacky stores were engaged in an ages-old competition that made Southport famous all up and down the coast. Every store had its own outrageous, gigantic model of a sea creature out in front, or four or five, to draw in the shoppers. CeeGee rode by one store with just the huge head of a shark in front, its wide-open jaw showing rows and rows of fearsome teeth. The shark's mouth was so big an entire family could stand inside for a vacation photo, which they did. CeeGee's twin brothers, Danny and Davey, could not go past the shark without leaping into its gaping mouth and pretending to die a violent death, until her parents told them to 'get out of that shark's mouth and get on over here, you boys.' Next was a school of leaping dolphins, then across the street an octopus so tall people could wander among its pink tentacles like a little forest. This was followed by a parade of gigantic, golden sea horses and down a few more doors a huge, blue shark that stretched twenty feet across the entry. Customers had to walk into the shark's mouth and out the back to get inside the store. Every time CeeGee's mother walked by this store she said, "What were these people thinking, making you walk through a shark's behind? Disgusting, simply disgusting."

Carl Williamson said that when he left his drugstore at closing time every day, he felt like he'd walked onto the set of an undersea fantasy movie and any minute someone would yell, "Okay, that's a wrap!" Then crews would come, load up all the outrageous props in big trucks, haul them away and Southport would look like a normal town. But this would never happen. Those sea creatures were what brought in the tourists and made Southport so special.

In pure defense, when Carl and Bobbie moved to the island from Seattle seventeen years before and bought the pharmacy, Carl had a great big new sign made to hang out front, high above the entry door. It said *Southport Sundries and Sodas*, the three words in red, stacked on top of each other with the S's real big. People used to call it the drugstore, but from then on everyone called it the Triple S. Carl would not go so far as putting a sea creature in front of his business, but he was going to have himself a sign that wouldn't be missed. That sign was the newest addition to Beacon Street for years.

CeeGee cut to the alley behind the store and parked her bike, then opened the metal service door she knew would be unlocked during business hours. She crossed the storage room, made her way through the aisles to the soda fountain and ordered her root beer float from Johnny Johanssen.

Johnny was a miserable looking kid. He slouched, and his hair stuck out every which way. He mumbled out of the side of his mouth and never, ever smiled. CeeGee knew all this because he had lived on her street since she was born, three years after her twin brothers. Johnny had been working at the Triple S ever since he landed in Bobbie's freshman English class and she decided this quiet, awkward and lonely student would feel better about himself if he had something to do besides go to high school—like a job at the Triple S. Carl didn't see why making Johnny Johanssen feel better about himself should be his problem, but Bobbie was determined, which was pretty nice of her, considering that when CeeGee was a baby Johnny whacked a baseball through their living room window. Bobbie, like usual, never gave up and Carl finally gave in.

Carl kept a hawk's eye on his new hire and at first, he just had Johnny clean up after the boy who worked the soda fountain. Johnny had to scrub and polish the dark gray Formica counter and the row of red vinyl stools. He had to wash and stack the little silver dishes with their pedestal bases in the shape of a pyramid on top of the bar. Then he had to line up the banana split dishes and soda glasses on a shelf, keep the sinks clean, and refill the ice cream containers from the freezer in the supply room.

Pretty soon, Johnny had everything in order and started experimenting with the ice cream recipes. Carl said the kid was so intense he reminded him of a scientist on the verge of a major discovery. One by one he made up trial dishes and offered them to Carl and old Mrs. Whiting who worked the cash register. It didn't take long for the two of them to realize that awkward and sullen Johnny Johanssen was a whiz at making absolutely perfect ice cream sodas, root beer floats, hot fudge sundaes and milk shakes. His banana splits were like works of art, with a scoop each of vanilla, chocolate and strawberry lined up neatly across the dish, whipped cream spooned over the top in lacy mounds and a big red cherry on the tip top. In time, he added a dusting of finely chopped pecans to make it his own.

Carl said, "You quit giving these to us for free, son. Start selling these to the customers!"

In six months, Johnny had a fan club and the kid who used to work the soda fountain was cleaning up after Johnny. Whole families came to the Triple S after church or fishing and ordered banana splits to share. Southport mothers came in with their toddlers for ice cream sundaes after a morning at the beach, and kids of all ages came after school for a milkshake or a float.

Johnny's dishes were so popular that Carl decided he better make the soda fountain bigger, so he took a whole aisle out of the sundries part of the store and put in a new row of five red vinyl-covered booths with gray Formica tabletops that matched the counter. Even with service for twenty more customers, it was still hard to get a seat in the soda fountain once it got hot outside. And, even though Johnny was a star, he stayed as sullen as ever.

CeeGee had to wait forever for Johnny to finally, finally bring her float. She didn't have to pay for it because her dad owned the store, and she never left Johnny a tip like some of the other customers, so it was no wonder he was slower and even more grumpy when he had to take care of her. She took her time sucking and slurping and licking her spoon and thinking about Mr. Tindale. By the time she twisted the straw in her glass to get to the last bits of foam on the bottom, she'd decided that instead of getting herself all worked up about her Knowing again, she'd go over to a tacky store and see if there were any tourists who wanted to get inside the shark's mouth, so she could take their family photo.

CeeGee called out a thank you to Johnny Johanssen behind the bar, waited for his usual gruff nod in reply, twirled off her stool and made her way to the front of the store. She gave her father a wave as she went past the pharmacy counter, said hello to Mrs. Whiting at the cash register and pulled open the big wooden door. No sooner had she stepped onto the sidewalk, but who did she see—strutting down Beacon in a clean white shirt, seersucker pants and a straw hat with a bright blue band—but Mr. Tindale!

When he caught sight of CeeGee, he raised his cane and pointed it at her. "Celia Gene Williamson! It is good to see you on this fine day."

"Mr. Tindale," CeeGee said as he approached her eagerly. "It's pretty hot today, isn't it?"

"Like I said, it's a fine day, and I'd say I'm lucky to be alive." He tapped the side of her sneaker with his cane, winked and said, "As you well know."

He looked so cheerful she figured maybe the midday heat had gotten to him and he forgot he was mad at her for telling him he didn't have much time left. CeeGee took his arm and pulled him into the shade under a store awning. "So, where you off to, dressed up so fancy?"

"I got a busy day," he said. "I got to go back to Sandwith Brothers' Funeral Home to check on my arrangements. I think I got everything all set. Still a few choices to make about the music, but those caskets—my land, they cost a pretty penny! At first, I thought I'd have an open casket, but after I looked them over with all the fancy gee-gaws—handles and hinges and satin and such—I thought, my land, no. They make 'em up to look like a brand-new car with frosted platinum paint. Silly if you ask me. Whatever happened to a simple box of good oak? That's what I'd go for if I could find...."

"Casket?"

"You know, the box I'll get buried in. What do you think?"

"About what?"

"About a plain wooden casket? Think I could get one made of oak and maybe line it myself with some nice fabric from the mainland? I got time for that, don't I? I'm not going to get hit by a truck tomorrow or anything, am I?"

For a moment, CeeGee was speechless. "Sure, I think you could do that, line it with fabric. And I'd, uh, I'd help if you want?"

"Why that would be fine, just fine." He cocked his head to the side, "You know I miss having you around, Celia Gene. And I should tell you, I'm sorry I got so mad at you. You just told me the plumb truth. Course I'm going to die, could be any time now, so might as well do it up right. But first, I have to find someone to make my box for me. Could take a while...you sure that's okay?"

"Yeah, sure. I think that's okay."

"All right, then. Well, good day, missy. I got a lot to do. I got to get on over to Sandwith Brothers, then I'm off to buy a new suit. Open casket, you know." He touched the brim of his hat and winked at her again.

CeeGee watched him as he walked away, whipping his cane around with each step like the drum major in a marching band. He had his chin up high and the rainbow of light she remembered from so long ago shimmered around his head once again. What had happened? A week ago, she gave Mr. Tindale her Knowing and he was furious. Today, he was acting like getting himself ready to die was a barrel of fun. And that pretty halo of light—did it come back, or was she just now able to see it? And how could she have given the worst Knowing of her whole entire life only to have the person who received the terrible news go strutting around like everything was plumb perfect?

CeeGee forgot all about the tacky stores and went straight back through the Triple S, got her bike from the alley and rode to the jetty. She needed to think.

Chapter Three

On the seaward side of Southport, the jetty stretches from the southeastern shore of the island out to the deeper gulf waters, creating a wide, calm channel to guide fishing boats and cargo ships safely to the mainland harbors. The jetty, made of huge cubes of rose-colored granite stacked on top of one another, is topped by an asphalt path. Most any day, a long line of fishermen stand all along the jetty, waving to the boats going by and casting into the channel while sand crabs scurry for lost bait among the granite rocks below. At the very end of the jetty the water is still and deep and the smell of civilization entirely absent, replaced by the scent of seaweed, hot stone and bright, briny water.

CeeGee rode her bike down Beach Road to the jetty and made sure to park in the dry sand above the high tide line. She climbed up the rocks to the path on top, stuffed her hands into her pockets, put her head down against the wind and started walking. She didn't even bother, like usual, to check on the fishermen to see what they had in their buckets. She didn't look down between the rocks in search of a crab or a sea urchin either; she just kept on walking out to the very end of the jetty, where rolling swells of slate-colored water slapped gently against salt-crusted stone. She found a block of granite positioned just right, sat down and got ready to work out all the questions that were tangled up in her mind. But before she could even get started, a voice interrupted.

"Mind if I join ya'?" CeeGee looked up into the glare of the sun and raised a hand to shield her eyes. Standing over her was Mike Robins, the carpenter who rebuilt the Williamsons' porch deck the summer before. "How you be, Celia Gene?"

"Hey, Mr. Robins, I'm okay." She pointed at the stone next to her, "Here, you want to have a seat?"

He shook his head 'no' without answering, which wasn't like him. Mike Robins was the kind of man who knew how to talk to a kid. When he was working on their house, CeeGee used to hang around until it was time for his break; then she'd bring him a big glass of ice water and sit with him while he drank it. He never shushed her or waved her away, and he always thought up interesting questions to ask her. After he got done for the day he would toss a ball around with Danny and Davey for a while, like he was the Dad of everyone. She remembered him as young looking and fit, but today his eyes were rimmed in red and his hair was shaggy and dirty, pulled back into a tangled wad that stuck out from under his baseball cap.

"What are you fishing for?" CeeGee asked.

Mike set down his gear, reached into his dirty shorts pocket and pulled out a plastic bait bag. "Dinner," he answered as he squatted down to bait the hook.

"Oh. Well, good luck."

"Yeah. Haven't had much of that lately." He stood, made his cast, waited a few seconds, then began to reel the line in, jerking and twisting his shoulders until the rod whipped back and forth over CeeGee's head.

He was upset, even a little scary, and CeeGee got to her feet thinking maybe she should leave, but before she had a chance to take a step away she felt the beam of light coming down, warming her skin. Again? Not another Knowing. She stayed put. "So, what's going on, Mr. Robins?"

"What ain't?" he said. "First off, the wife got sick right after she had our last kid, the fourth. We couldn't afford the kid in the first place. I mean, I love him and all, but he was an accident, you know, and we needed the wife to go back to work to make ends meet, but she got so sick she couldn't. Top a' that, I got laid off a few months back; then the boss went broke 'fore he could hire me back. I'm just tryin' to hang on to our house; that's how bad things are."

"Hey, sorry to hear all that. What a streak of bad luck."

"It's a damn mess, that's what it is. Oh, sorry, I shouldn't a' said that. No damned excuse for cussin' in front of a kid. Shoot, did it again. Sorry 'bout that."

"That's okay. How's your wife feeling now?"

"Sicker." Mike reeled in his line and saw the bait was gone, which was no surprise with all of his jerking and twisting. CeeGee stood by him in silence as he re-baited his hook and made another cast. The light kept on coming and CeeGee began to get the gist of her Knowing.

"Say, Mr. Robins…"

"Call me Mike, for Christ's sake…sorry."

"Okay then, Mike. What would you really like to do, if you could do anything you wanted?"

"Win the lottery."

"No, I mean for a job."

He looked over at her and once he saw it was a serious question he put down his pole, sat down on the block of granite and hung his forearm across his knee. CeeGee sat next to him and waited. "Furniture. I always wanted to make wooden furniture, ever since I can remember. But, no one makes custom furniture 'round here, so there was nobody to work for and I was too scared to go out on my own. Besides, look at this town, whadda' we have, a few thousand people? And most of 'em not in much better shape than I am. How many people you think would order a one-of-a-kind piece of furniture? Maybe a coffee table made from a surfboard or somethin' like that, but not enough so's I could support my family proper. Top of that, seemed like every time I'd start in dreamin' about starting up my own business, there'd be another new kid at home, hungry as a baby bird, mouth wide open all the time. Never was any extra money to tide us over. Anyway, long story short, make furniture—that's what I always wanted to do…like you asked."

"I guess you haven't got much to lose right now, huh?"

He plucked a dried-up piece of bait off a rock and flipped it into the water like a cigarette butt and laughed dryly. "I got nothin', so yeah, guess I got nothin' to lose."

They sat silently for a long time, staring out at the rolling swells while CeeGee tried to sort out where her Knowing was taking her. Finally, the pieces came together, and she could see the connections as clear as a constellation in the sky. "Mr. Robins, do you think a casket counts as furniture?"

"A casket, nah." He shook his head, then stopped and thought for a moment. "Well…yeah…I guess it could, with some good wood and the hardware and joinery and all. Kind of like a fancy extra-long trunk. Why, somebody die?"

"It'd be for Mr. Tindale."

"No kiddin'? That's a shame. I'm real sorry to hear that. Why, I just saw old Tindale in town the other day. He looked just fine to me, fit as a fiddle."

"He's not dead yet. He just wants the casket for when he is. Dead, I mean."

"How the hell would you know that? Sorry."

"He's my friend. He told me."

"Seems mighty strange." Mike Robins thought for a few moments longer. "Other hand, come to think of it, maybe with his wife gone and all that's the way to do it. Take care of things 'fore it happens. Yeah, that'd be good, making a casket. I'll go talk to him."

"Let me talk to him first. I'll do it right now. Then you can go—maybe early in the morning?" CeeGee stood to leave, then added, "He wants it to be oak."

"All right, I'll do that, I'll get on over there first thing."

CeeGee ran all the way back down the jetty, pedaled her bike as fast as she could to Mr. Tindale's house and told him that Mike Robins would make his casket and that he would come over to talk about it first thing in the morning. CeeGee said she was pretty sure she could get permission from her Mom to go to the mainland to buy the satin casket lining, so they decided as soon as Mr. Tindale was finished with Mike, they would head out.

Mr. Tindale rubbed his hands together and said, "This is good, a good plan, thanks for helping me out with it. You get on home now, girl. I don't want your momma gettin' mad at me."

Before she left, CeeGee said, "Mr. Tindale, Mike's come on some real hard times. He's out of work and his wife's awful sick, so this will really help him out." Mr. Tindale gave her a smile, "Nice of you to notice and to care, Celia Gene. You do have that special way about you, child." He reached out and squeezed her shoulder.

When CeeGee got home, she found her mother at the stove fixing dinner. "Hey, Momma."

Her mother put down her spatula, stepped over and lifted CeeGee's hair off her damp neck with both hands and kissed her on the cheek. "Hey darlin'. Did you have a good day?"

"I did, Momma, I had a real good day," CeeGee said. "Thanks for kicking me out of the house this morning."

"You are most welcome. Where all did you go? To the marsh?" Bobbie turned back to the stove and used her spatula to lift the corner of a fish fillet. The underside was golden brown with flecks of burnt black in it like bits of confetti. She flipped the fish over gently.

"Not today, Momma, but I'll get to the marsh soon. Today I went to the Triple S for a float like you said. And I went out on the jetty, and I saw Mike Robins. I saw Mr. Tindale too, and he invited me to go shopping on the mainland with him. We'd take his car and go across on the ferry. He wants to go tomorrow. Can I, Momma?"

Bobbie turned back to her daughter and smiled gently, "I think that would be fine. Be nice for you to keep him company," she said. "Besides, it'll get you out of the house for two whole days in a row. Might become a habit. What else did you do?"

"That's about it, Momma."

Bobbie opened a can of stewed tomatoes. "Then you go on and clean up. Dinner's almost ready and you're sticky all over."

"Okay. What all's for dinner?"

"I've got this catfish, and I'm making fried okra with tomatoes. Mashed potatoes and biscuits are already in the oven."

"That sounds good, Momma, really good." CeeGee watched her mother put flour, cornmeal, salt and pepper into a paper bag.

Bobbie added the okra to the bag, rolled the top closed, held the bag up high and shook it a few times. She did the little dance she always did, like she was shaking a Maraca in a Mariachi band, then bumped CeeGee with her hip, "Get on now, Celia Gene, you'll be late. And tell your brothers to wash up for dinner."

That night after dinner was over, it was the twins turn to clear the table and CeeGee's to clean up the kitchen. By the time she was done, everyone had gone off to their rooms. CeeGee needed to think, so she went to her bedroom and changed into her nightgown. Then she went quietly back down the hall, crossed the living room and opened the kitchen door to the deck.

Just as she was about to step out, she heard a thumping sound. She knew it well. Danny and Davey were throwing a tennis ball against their bedroom wall over and over as they wound down the day. She could see them, sitting side by side on a twin bed. Danny throws one across the room, thump against the wall, bounce on the floor, Davey catches. Davey throws one across the room, thump against the wall, bounce on the floor, Danny catches. Then she waited for the next inevitable scene in this oft-repeated movie.

"You boys!" she heard her father yell from his bedroom. "Put away that damn ball and go to sleep!" One more thump and then the finale. "You hear me? Another sound from you two and I'm coming down there."

"Yeah, Dad."

"Sorry, Dad."

Would they never learn? CeeGee went outside and quietly closed the door behind her, crossed the deck and went down the stairs to the backyard. She climbed onto the wooden swing hanging from the tree and began to rock back and forth, back and forth. Finally, she quieted down enough to think about what had happened. She'd had a pretty good day, no doubt about it. And the reason for it was her two Knowings, no doubt about that either. The terrible one about Mr. Tindale hadn't happened at all. The other one, about better times coming for Mike Robins, looked to be good news all around—for Mike, his family and even Mr. Tindale in a way. Plus, it was all connected—the bad news for Mr. Tindale led straight to the good news for Mike Robins. How could that be? If there was one thing CeeGee knew for sure it was that her Knowings were always bad. They always came true and always brought nothing but trouble. She'd spent the past three long, lonely years doing her best to keep them from coming. Now she'd had two in a week and there was no trouble in sight.

What should she do? Was this just the moment of calm before the bad storm that would wreck everything? Or had something changed with her and with the Knowings? She couldn't talk to her parents about it—that was out. She'd learned that much when she was nine. And unlike her brothers, she was not about to keep stirring up trouble with her parents, over and over again.

CeeGee looked up at the sky, exhausted from remembering. She was afraid, afraid of the bright light that brought the Knowings, afraid of what she would come to know, afraid of the harm that might come to someone. She searched the sky for the constellations, trying to remember how the special stars were laid out in the heavens above. If she could just connect the right stars, one to another, there would be a picture in the sky, instead of bits of light and patches of darkness scattered everywhere. If she searched, maybe she could see Scorpio, or The Big and Little Dipper like her Dad taught her. Right now, she was all in a tangle, wary of the present, tired of the past. But maybe there could be a way to connect all this—the things that happened years ago and the things that were happening now. Perhaps it could all make up a picture, like a constellation in the stars, and she could find a way to make sense of it and go on. Maybe she didn't have to go back to where she had been, stay forever the person she had decided to be at nine years old, locked up inside, connected to no one. Maybe she could travel into today, shoot into the unknown and become someone else, the person who knew Mr. Tindale was going to die, and the person who knew Mike Robins was going to have a better life. And maybe it could be all right for her to know both of these things.

After staring at the heavens for a while longer and trying to make meaning out of the vast, brightly lit sky and where she might fit in that design, she still didn't have a thing sorted out. Her Knowings were back, whether she liked it or not, and she didn't want things to turn out bad like they had before. She couldn't talk to her parents because they just wanted a nice normal kid and that's what she aimed to be, as far as they were concerned. And she couldn't figure out any of this on her own, that was for sure. Finally, she decided that tomorrow she would take a chance and talk to Mr. Tindale about it. He had that rainbow of light shimmering around his head, maybe there was a chance he would be able to understand and help.

Chapter Four

C eeGee got up early the next morning, ate a bowl of cereal and rode over to Mr. Tindale's. She parked her bike by the garage in back and went around to the front porch where she could hear Mr. Tindale talking with Mike Robins through the screen. She let herself in quietly.

"Mahogany is the wood," Mike said. "Fine grained, deep in color. Would make a proper casket for a gentleman like yourself."

"Oak. Not for debate," Mr. Tindale said as he caught sight of CeeGee. "Hello there, Celia Gene." He turned back to Mike, "Let's talk about the hardware."

"Well, if it has to be oak, then I think we should go with an antique finish."

"Not too fancy, I want simple and plain."

"Then how about a Shaker effect, that's about as plain as it gets? I can probably find some handles in a burnished bronze."

"Now we're getting somewhere," Mr. Tindale pulled out his wallet and started counting out bills. "All right, young man, Celia Gene and I have to be off to the mainland to find that satin lining—baby blue to match the stripes in my new suit. We'll buy padding too, so it'll be nice and comfortable." He handed Mike several bills. "You sure you can teach us how to put that lining in proper? I don't want my resting place to look too homemade. Still, I want to do Maggie May proud that I lined it myself and all."

"No problem there at all." Mike counted out the money. "This is too much, sir. I just need enough to buy materials."

"Go on, take it. It's a deposit. I want you working on a full stomach."

Mike looked down at the handful of bills. "This will help. It will help a lot."

"Since you're so flush, why don't you get yourself a haircut while you're at it," Mr. Tindale said.

"Yes, sir, I'll do that, I surely will. I want to thank you for this... for the work." Mike turned away quickly and made for the door.

After Mike left, Mr. Tindale went out the back door and pulled his car out of the garage, CeeGee got in and they drove to the ferry landing without speaking. When the ferry attendant waved at them, they drove on to the big flat boat, Mr. Tindale turned off the engine and CeeGee got out of the car to lean against the rail as they made the crossing. When they pulled away from the landing, a flock of squawking gulls and three or four dolphins joined them and escorted the ferry across the channel. They did this all day long, back and forth, like it was their life's work.

CeeGee loved her island home, the way its shores were embroidered with so many patterns–the arc of pale golden beaches bordered by vine-laced dunes. The muted shallows of the sandbars, the muddy tidal flats, gray bays, salty ponds and her favorite, the dense grassy marsh. The marsh was on the inland side of the island bordering the channel and as they crossed, she could see the calm waters and the shallow inlets in the distance. She knew that deeper into the marsh were high swaying grasses and a wondrous assortment of birds—from long-legged herons to tiny terns, from orioles, cormorants and egrets, to the same pelicans that squatted on the pilings at the ferry docks. Some of the birds lived on the island year-round, others came and went with the time of day or the seasons of the year. CeeGee knew them all by name and when to go and visit them.

As they approached the mainland dock, CeeGee got back in the car.

"So, did you enjoy your crossing, young lady?"

"I did, I always do," CeeGee answered. She was nervous about talking to Mr. Tindale today, but making the crossing had helped her calm down and get herself ready.

Mr. Tindale waited for the attendant to wave them off and they drove to the first stoplight where they sat, listening to the loud click, click, click, of his turn signal. "So, I'm thinking we go to the store and get the fabric, and then have us a good mainland lunch before we head back home. How's that sound?"

"That sounds good, Mr. Tindale. Think we could go to Smithy's for lunch?"

"Well, child, you read my mind. That was my thought exactly." Mr. Tindale took a right turn and they drove further away from the island, the landscape changing from the broad sidewalks, tacky stores and sea creatures of Beacon Street to big billboards and plain cinder block buildings facing a four-lane highway. They couldn't see any street names or numbers, so they both watched out the window for the sign on the fabric store they knew was somewhere along the left side of the road. By the time they saw it, they had missed the turnoff and had to take the next exit, cross over the highway and double back. Mr. Tindale wasn't used to a lot of traffic or stoplights, so CeeGee stayed quiet and let him concentrate.

Once they arrived, Mr. Tindale drove round and round the huge parking lot, honked at a few cars and dodged a shopper before he found an empty spot. When they finally made it into the air-conditioned building, Mr. Tindale pulled out his white handkerchief, wiped off his face and said, "Makes you glad you live on a pint-sized island, don't it?"

It didn't take them any time at all to find the perfect baby blue satin, and it was even on a mark down sale. Mr. Tindale turned his back to CeeGee and said, "Child, hold the edge of that fabric up to here." He pointed to the top of his head.

"What for?"

"So's we can measure how much we need. I figure if we get my height and add another couple feet or so for each end, we'll be set."

CeeGee did as she was told, but when she pulled up on the end, the whole bolt of fabric fell off the shelf and landed on the floor with a loud thud. This brought an employee over.

"May I help you here?" the lady said, like it was an accusation. She picked up the bolt from the floor and began to wrap it back up, brushing off the fabric and clucking. CeeGee stood there holding her end as if the two of them were folding a flag. When the lady took the last of the fabric out of her hands, she gave CeeGee a disapproving look just like Miss McGuire at the library would do. "Now, how can I assist you?" she said, turning to speak to Mr. Tindale.

"Actually, we were doing just fine on our own," he said, "but since you're here, we need fabric as tall as me with a few feet extra."

"It is customary to use yards rather than feet to measure fabric." The lady looked down her nose at Mr. Tindale, then pulled a measuring tape out of her apron pocket. "If you'd turn around." She pointed to the floor and made a little swirling motion with her finger.

Mr. Tindale turned his back to her. "My pleasure," he said in a voice just as snotty as hers. "I'm guessing we'll need about two and a half yards then, give or take."

She stretched the tape from the top of his head, marked her place at his waist, then squatted down and stretched it again to his feet. She stood back up and pulled a tiny tablet out of her apron pocket. "So, what are you making with this lovely fabric? Seems a mite feminine for a big man like you."

CeeGee couldn't wait to hear. She went to stand in front of Mr. Tindale and raised both eyebrows.

He didn't miss a beat. "Why, my lovely wife is quite tall, taller even than I am. In order for my little friend to make her the gift of a, uh, nightdress, I'm the model." He winked at CeeGee. Then he had to start embellishing. "Celia Gene is taking a sewing class this summer, and, umm, my dear, dear wife took a bad fall, she did, and broke her leg and is now stuck in bed." He made a fake sad face, and patted CeeGee on top of her head, "This will be such a nice surprise."

"Why that is lovely, simply lovely," the saleslady said as she pulled a pencil out of her apron pocket, licked the tip and started writing. "Let's see, this fabric is fifty-four inches wide, so I think you will have plenty—fabric to spare, if we cut you three yards. Do you have your pattern with you, dear? That way we could be sure." She leaned around Mr. Tindale to look at CeeGee.

"No, ma'am, I forgot it," CeeGee said as they moved to the cutting table.

The woman made another disapproving cluck as she rolled out the fabric on the table, brushing away the dust bunnies from the floor and adding an extra cluck every time she found one. "Now," she said when she was finished cutting, "is there anything else I can help you with?"

"Oh, yes. That reminds me," CeeGee said, "we need some quilt batting, too."

"Are you also making a quilt in your class? Goodness, that's quite an advanced project for a child your age. But, no mind, I can show you our selection of quilt fabrics. We have quite an array, if I do say so myself."

CeeGee glanced at Mr. Tindale for help, but he grinned back at her without saying a word. "I, uh, already have lots of fabric. I've been collecting. And, uh, Mrs. Tindale happens to be an expert quilter. Even though she's stuck in bed, she said she can help teach me to quilt."

"Oh my, that's very kind of the poor dear. All right then, let's have a look at the batting. We have several weights."

"We want the softest one." Mr. Tindale said firmly. "And the thickest."

"I can see the quilt is going to be for you then, sir." CeeGee elbowed Mr. Tindale as they walked behind the saleslady. "All right, the heaviest weight would be this one here. And how many yards do we need?"

"The same," CeeGee and Mr. Tindale said in unison.

"As the satin?" the saleslady asked. "Why that won't be enough, you see you have to have enough to cover the sides of the bed, you'd need double that, I'd say."

"It's a throw," Mr. Tindale said and turned to walk back to the cutting table. "The same amount will work just fine."

When they finally got out of the fabric store with their purchases, Mr. Tindale opened the car door and said, "I've never done so much fabricating about fabric in all my born days. Let's go have lunch."

They drove to Smithy's Family Cafeteria, CeeGee's very most favorite place to go out to eat. Sometimes the Williamsons came over to the mainland just to go to Smithy's because they were open all day long, had a huge selection of the best food anywhere, and everyone in the family got exactly what they wanted. Every time she went to Smithy's, CeeGee had to read every item that was posted on the menu board—twice. Then she had to walk down the cafeteria line to make sure each one matched the description on the wall exactly. Then, after all that fuss, she almost always got the same meal, with a double on the desserts. That was the great thing about a cafeteria; she could get two of anything, if her parents would let her. CeeGee knew that by being at Smithy's with a good meal and a nice private booth, she would be able to settle down and tell Mr. Tindale her story.

She let Mr. Tindale go through the line first. He got roast chicken, mashed potatoes, peas, an iced tea to drink and strawberry shortcake for dessert. CeeGee got her usual—rainbow trout, French fries, Jello with whipped cream, lemon meringue pie and a lemonade. Mr. Tindale paid for both of them. He stepped away from the cash register, holding his tray and looking around for a table, his cane looped over his arm. CeeGee saw an open booth on the far wall by a window and nodded toward it, he nodded in return and hobbled over. CeeGee waited while he put down his tray, hung his cane on the coat rack behind the booth and sat down. She emptied both their trays, setting the napkins, plates, side dishes, silverware and glasses neatly on the table, one by one. Then she moved the trays to the empty table next to them and sat down in the booth across from him.

She didn't waste any time getting to what was on her mind. "Mr. Tindale, I need to talk to you about some things, important things. Would it be all right to do that now?"

"Sure," he said as he unfolded his napkin, placing it in his lap. "Tell me what's on your mind, child. Errands are done, so we got all day." He took a sip of tea, looked over at her and grinned, "Least I hope so."

CeeGee returned a weak smile, then took a breath. "Okay. You know that day in the garden when I told you that you didn't have much time left, that your time was short?"

"Hard to forget that message," he said as he began cutting into his chicken.

"Well, that was what I call a Knowing. I had one there in your garden."

"You had a what?" Mr. Tindale stopped and looked back at her, fork in mid-air.

"A Knowing. It's when a light comes down from over my head, like a bright beam, and then it goes into me, and all of the sudden I know things." CeeGee took a took a sip of her lemonade and waited for his reaction.

Mr. Tindale leaned back against the booth and laid his hands on the table. "What kinds of things?" he asked.

"I know things that are going to happen—before they actually happen."

He leaned back toward her, "Celia Gene, are you playing around with me? I didn't see no beam of light down there in the garden that day."

"I don't think anyone can see the light but me." CeeGee pushed her glasses up on her nose, leaned toward him and said seriously, "And no, sir, I am not playing around with you. The light and the Knowings—that's the thing I need to talk to you about."

Mr. Tindale kept staring at her hard. "So, this what-you-call-it, a Knowing? This is why you told me my time was short and all?"

"Yes, sir."

"Well, I'll be," he said, scooping up a bite of mashed potatoes. After a long pause, he shook his head and said, "Celia Gene, now listen here, I am an old man, and my time *is* short. Anyone can see it. It did make me a little testy to have some child telling me to get my affairs in order, but it was high time for me to start making my plans for leaving this here earth." He stopped speaking and thought a moment as he cut another piece of chicken. "So, there it is," he declared. "I don't think you should be making too much of this, and I'm sorry if I made you feel like I blamed you or something for tellin' me what you did." Then he pointed at her napkin beside her plate and gave her a look.

CeeGee took the napkin and dropped it to her lap. "Mr. Tindale, that's not it. I know you aren't mad at me anymore, and I know you care about me. That's why I think you're the one I need to talk to about all this." She looked down and paused for a moment before she said, "You see…that was not my first Knowing."

"Well, that would cast a different light on things," he replied. "All right then, you best tell me all about these Knowings of yours." He sat back and straightened his napkin in his lap.

CeeGee collected herself, took a bite of her pie and chewed slowly. It had been so long since she talked about her Knowings. It was against her rules. Who knew what might happen? She could get hit by lightning right there in the diner. She leaned over to the window and looked up at the sky to see if any clouds were gathering.

Mr. Tindale leaned out the same direction and looked up, too. Then he positioned his face in front of hers and caught her eye. "Celia Gene, you go on now. You don't have to be scared. I'm right here, listening hard."

CeeGee straightened back up and started in. "Well, first of all, you know how I told you Mike Robins was coming over to talk about building your casket?" Mr. Tindale nodded. "Well, I sent him to you because I had a Knowing about him, too. I knew that even though he lost his job and times were tough, he didn't have to find another job. Building things on his own is going to be his future. It's going to change everything for him and his family."

"It did seem a coincidence that he showed up right when I needed him."

"It was no coincidence," CeeGee said, "not at all."

"So, this Knowing you had about good old Mike, it seems like good news, that things will get better for him. Like you held the door open for a man who needed it."

"It does seem like that, this time."

"Then, why are you so worried about these Knowings of yours?"

"Like I said, this time it did seem like good news, but not all the other times. It's been so awful, Mr. Tindale. My Knowings have been the worst news in the world."

"Other times?"

"Yes."

"Worse news, like mine? Like someone was fixin' to die?"

"Exactly. That someone was about to die or get hurt real bad." CeeGee looked up at him and glared. "And it's all my fault, don't you see?"

"Whoa, that was a quick turn." Mr. Tindale lifted his napkin and wiped off his mouth before placing it back across his lap. "Okay," he went on, "I think you need to go all the way back to the beginning and tell me your whole story."

CeeGee nodded, spooned a bite of Jello and held it up, the red cube quivering in her hand. "I will. I'll tell you the whole story," she said.

Chapter Five

"The first time I had a Knowing," CeeGee began, "well actually, the first one I can remember, was when I was about four years old. I was walking down Beacon with my family and we were on our way out to dinner." CeeGee leaned across the table and lowered her voice, "All of a sudden, this light comes down over my head, and I start swatting at it, like I have bees on me or something. But the light gets in, and I run across the parking lot of the Shop and Save, straight for this lady. I grab her around the knees, crying and saying, 'Sorry, Sorry, Sorry,' until my dad pulls me off her."

"What was it that you knew?" Mr. Tindale asked.

"Well, I didn't know the lady, I just knew something really sad was going to happen for her. It turned out she was Mrs. Jennings, you know, the secretary down at the Presbyterian Church?"

"Yes, I know who you mean." Mr. Tindale nodded as he used his knife to load some peas onto his fork.

"And do you remember that her husband dropped dead of a heart attack?"

"Ahhh, yes, I do remember that." Mr. Tindale chewed as he nodded, then said, "He was a pretty young fella'."

"Right, and they had a couple of little kids."

"So, do you think that grabbing her and saying sorry, sorry was because you knew Mr. Jennings was about to die?"

"Yes." CeeGee answered.

"And this was the first one?"

"This was the first time that I acted on what I knew, but as far back as I can remember I've had this feeling I'm like a radio, picking up signals going by. Not that I can hear them or anything, it's more like I feel them, like they hum into me. This time the hum became a beam of light coming straight in to me, and the radio got into tune. I was too little to know exactly what the Knowing was telling me, I just knew it was sad for her."

"I can almost see it, child, I can almost feel it myself." He shook his head slowly at the thought. "So, you were with your folks, right? What did they do when this happened, besides your dad pulling you away from her?"

"They didn't fit it together. My mom told me later that when she heard about Mr. Jennings' heart attack, she had a tickle in her memory, but she was too damned tired to scratch at it."

"Not surprising, what with her teaching job and raising you and those rascally brothers of yours." Mr. Tindale pushed some mashed potatoes through the gravy on his plate. "So, what happened next?"

"So, the humming kept on, but it wasn't until a year or so later that the light came down again and I got the next awful Knowing." CeeGee paused, wishing she did not have to go back to that time. Finally, she said softly, "Mr. Tindale. It was Kenny Keller."

"Awww, Kenny the Paperboy. I still miss him."

"I miss Kenny, too," she whispered.

"I'm sure you do. Kenny was special."

"He was." CeeGee smiled slightly at her memories and said, "I remember when he came by at Christmas, my dad always gave him a big tip."

"Your dad and everyone else. Kenny was the best-paid paperboy in all of Southport," Mr. Tindale smiled back at her. "I'll never forget the sight of him weaving down the street on his three-wheeler. Good thing he stayed on that bike most of the time, 'cause he could barely walk."

"And barely talk. When he came to the door at Christmas, he'd always say, 'I am heah for my Cwisthmus tip.' Mr. Tindale, did you ever know what was wrong with Kenny, why he couldn't walk and talk right?"

"Never did, never cared, just knew he was born that way." Mr. Tindale looked over at CeeGee who had lost her smile and was dragging her spoon through the whipped cream on top of the Jello. He reached over and touched her arm. "Now, child, don't you be sad. These are good memories. Kenny had a fine life, thanks to his saint of a mother and a town that loved him just the way he was. You go on with your story now."

"Okay." CeeGee took a breath and tried to shake her sadness away. "Here's how the Knowing happened. Kenny's twenty-second birthday was coming up and I made him a gift, like I did every year. That year I made him a card that said, *Happy Birthday, Kenny. Please wave to me from heaven.*"

"Oh boy. How old were you?"

"I was seven, in second grade. So, my mom read the card and just figured that I'd picked up on how Mrs. Keller used to talk about Kenny, how she said he was an angel, with one foot on earth and the other one in heaven."

"She did love that boy. But wait, did you have a Knowing, with the light and all?"

"Yes, but this time it was soft and peaceful coming in. I knew that's what it should say when I sat down to make him the card. I remember my mom felt funny about giving Kenny the card, so she suggested we make some fudge and take that to him on his birthday." CeeGee paused and looked out the window, lost in memories.

"That weekend, my mom was making breakfast for me, Danny and Davey when we heard this loud siren. The twins jumped up and took off after it on their bikes, with my mom yelling out the door after them to be careful. When she turned back to me, I was waving up at the ceiling, real sweet-like. Then I said, 'Hey there, Kenny.'"

"So, you knew what was going to happen to Kenny?"

"I knew it already had."

"Oh my, how'd you feel about that? Did you feel like he was waving back at you, like the card said?"

CeeGee finished chewing a bite of pie, then said, "Well, I didn't feel sad, like I did with Mrs. Jennings. And even though I loved Kenny like everyone did, I wasn't torn up. I just felt like, there's our Kenny, passing on through. Give him a wave."

"Interesting. Wonder why that was?"

"Why what was?"

"Why you felt so different this time."

"I don't know, Mr. Tindale. I have no idea why any of this happens the way it does. Or why I feel the way I do. That's what I need you to help me figure out."

"Right, I'll do my best." He reached over and moved her pie and Jello to the center of the table and pushed the lunch plate in front of her. "But, while I'm at it, let's get you on to your actual meal—now that you've nearly finished both desserts."

CeeGee shrugged, picked up the ketchup, loaded a big puddle next to the fries and went on. "Okay, so my brothers got to the accident right after the ambulance and they saw Kenny lying there beside that big ole' rock, with his head bleeding and his three-wheeler stuck in a ditch. He was already gone. They came hauling back home crying and blubbering."

"And this time, did your parents figure out that you knew what was going to happen?"

"No, they just got sad, like the rest of Southport. Mom was busy helping Mrs. Keller with the funeral and came home crying every night."

"I remember, we were all mute with grief," Mr. Tindale said, shaking his head. "No one talked on the street for days."

"No one came into the soda fountain at the Triple S either. It was like they felt guilty treating themselves to anything nice with Kenny gone and all."

"But, that funeral your momma helped plan? It was beautiful, just what we all needed." Mr. Tindale stared into space for a moment, lost in his own memories. "All right child, enough of my blathering. Is there more?"

"There's one more, a really bad one."

"I can take it, child, just keep on."

"Okay. You know Ronnie Sampson, right?"

"Who doesn't? That boy was nothing but trouble—until that car accident put him in a wheelchair. Oh my, his car accident. I think I might know where this one is going."

"Yes, you probably do." CeeGee looked at the three French fries in her hand, laid them back on her plate and wiped her hand with her napkin. "So, before the accident happened, my mom and I were in town one day to go shopping for school clothes. We had just started to cross the street when Ronnie came screeching around the corner in his car and nearly hit us. My mother yanked me back to the curb and started yelling after him and shaking her fist. You know how she would do, 'You blankety-blank boy! Someone is going to get hurt one of these days.'"

"I can hear her clear as day," Mr. Tindale said with a fond smile.

"Right then, the light flashed into me and I had a Knowing. I took her hand and said, 'Yes, Momma, Ronnie's going to get hurt real bad.' I remember she stopped yelling after him and looked down at me sort of puzzled. I knew that even though Ronnie was always getting into trouble, my momma felt bad for him, with no father at home and a mother who couldn't take charge of him. So, then I felt bad for her. I reached up and touched her face and said I hoped that Ronnie would be careful, so no one would get hurt at all."

"How old were you for this one?"

"It was the summer before fourth grade, so I was nine."

"That would mean, after Kenny, no Knowings for nearly two years?"

"I think there were almost a few. Like I said, sometimes I could feel the hum in the air, the radio trying to come into tune, but after Kenny, I didn't really want to let it in." CeeGee stopped talking, cut a piece of fish and swirled it in the tartar sauce on her plate.

"What, child?"

"Mr. Tindale, I didn't do anything to help."

"What could you have done?"

She looked up at him, "I knew. I could have warned Ronnie."

"You were a mere child. Besides, it wasn't just Ronnie, he was part of that whole gang of ruffians, all of 'em heading for nothing but trouble. A nine-year-old child was not going to stop those boys."

"Still."

CeeGee dropped her head again and Mr. Tindale reached over and squeezed her shoulder. "What? Go on now, tell me what's hurtin' your heart so bad."

"Can't you see? That's three people who got hurt or died, and I knew all three were going to happen. But I didn't do anything, I didn't warn anyone. What kind of a person does that make me?"

"That makes you a very young girl, with a mysterious gift that you don't understand and didn't ask for."

"But still."

"Still nothing. Let's just try to understand this gift of yours, then maybe we can figure out how to give it proper."

"Gift? Why do you keep calling it that? How can knowing these awful things are going to happen, and doing nothing about it, be called a gift? I'd call it more of a curse." CeeGee took a bite of her fish and chewed slowly before she went on. "I remember after the accident, watching while my dad helped to build the wheelchair ramp at Ronnie's house, the same way my mom helped with Kenny's funeral. Every day I saw Ronnie get more and more alone in that chair. When the men were done building the ramp, Ronnie didn't even use it, he didn't leave the house. He just locked himself up and stayed inside."

"Yes, and I remember most of his troublemaker friends left the island for one reason or another. It was like that car accident was an ending."

"It was for me, too. After Ronnie, I didn't want to ever have another Knowing. I didn't want the light to come. I just locked up, same as Ronnie. I didn't want to go anywhere or do anything. Not even fishing with my dad or tagging along with my brothers. After a while, my parents got called into the school because I changed so much. They said I wasn't raising my hand or participating in class. In the cafeteria, I had my head in a book and was eating by myself. I've always been kind of quiet with other kids at school, but they said this was more."

"This breaks my heart, Celia Gene, truly it does." Mr. Tindale wiped his face with his napkin.

"I know, it's really hard." She waited until he put the napkin back in his lap. "So, my parents came home from the meeting and tried to talk to me, but I wouldn't. I know now that they were just trying to be nice, asking what was on my mind, asking if I needed help with my studies, or if I had a problem with a kid at school. But I was too closed up. I was so afraid something else would happen with a Knowing, like it did with Ronnie. Deep down I was afraid I'd get a bad Knowing about one of my parents, or my brothers, and I would just stand by and do nothing all over again until someone in my family had their life ruined. Because of me."

"You poor, poor child; this is too great a burden for a young girl to bear," Mr. Tindale said as CeeGee lifted her glasses and wiped at her eyes. "Celia Gene, we can stop if remembering all this is too hard."

"No, I have to tell you the whole thing, Mr. Tindale. I have to find a way to make sense of this and you're the only one I can think of who might be able to help."

"Why do you think that?"

"I guess it's because when I had the Knowing about you, it just came so fast I couldn't keep it out. At first, I thought it was another bad one, another death in Southport. But then you told me it was all right, it was something you needed to hear. And then straight away I had the Knowing about Mike Robins, which connects to yours and should be good for him. That's never happened before. So somehow, for the first time, instead of just one awful tragedy after another, these two Knowings are connected one to the other, like in the stars, like they are part of a pattern that was meant to be. That makes me think you are the person who can help me. Maybe you are my guide to understanding that pattern. Maybe I can let the Knowings come back, and they won't all have to be bad."

"I'll do my best, child, I promise you." Mr. Tindale swiped at his face with the napkin again before he continued. "But I have an idea, if you're done with your eating here, let's get out of this place and head on back to the ferry. We can talk more on the way home, being on the water might make things easier for you." He laid his napkin on the table. "That sound okay with you?"

"Yes, sir, I think that would be good." CeeGee picked up her napkin and wiped her eyes. "The water would be good," she said.

Chapter Six

They rode to the ferry landing in silence, both lost in their own thoughts. Once Mr. Tindale got the car in line, he turned to her and said, "All right, child, did you have a chance to catch your breath? Think you can keep on with your story now?"

"Yes, sir, I think so." She shifted in her seat to face him. "So, like I said back at Smithy's, my parents had talked to the school and tried to talk to me, and when I wouldn't tell them anything I thought maybe they'd just let it go. But you know how my mom is, she never gives up. After the meeting, she got herself quiet and went back through my whole life, each thing that happened to me, and finally she pieced it all together."

"Your momma is a smart lady. And I know she loves you more than anything."

"I know that, too, Mr. Tindale. So, after she got it all figured out, she sat my dad down and made him listen while she took him through the whole thing. She told him she had started out by re-membering Ronnie, how it was right after his accident that I went silent and things went bad at school. She told him how just a few days before Ronnie's accident I said he was going to get hurt real bad. She went back to Kenny and the card I made asking him to wave to me from heaven, and then how I waved goodbye to him before anyone knew what had happened. She told my dad about that tickle in her memory after Mr. Jennings died and how I said

'Sorry, sorry' to Mrs. Jennings in that parking lot, weeks before her husband passed away.

"She even remembered another time when I was just a toddler. She said I was in my bed for a nap and I woke up crying and yelling for her to come to me. She ran from the living room into my room. Just as she picked me up, she heard a big crash. She carried me back to the living room and there was a baseball rolling across the floor, right where she'd been standing. The living room window was broken to bits and there was glass everywhere. She told my dad, I reached up to her face and said, 'No boo-boo's, Momma.'"

"Celia Gene, I have to ask, how do you know about all this talk between your parents?"

"I couldn't sleep that night, and I heard their voices in the dining room. I got up and stood in the hall, listening to them."

"And, your momma never made any of these connections before this night?"

"No, even with the one when I was a baby, she said she was so mad when she looked out the window and realized that Johnny Johanssen had slammed the baseball through the window that, right then, all she could think about was making him pay. After she had gone through the whole thing, reminding my dad of each one, she said she thought there were a few too many times I knew things before they happened for it all to be a coincidence."

"That would be quite a lot for your dad to take in. What did he say?"

"Well, at first Dad said he thought it *was* all just a coincidence. He argued back that maybe I just had real strong, what's that word, *in to* something...?"

"Intuition?"

"Right. He said I had always been sensitive that way and my mom was making too much of it. But she wouldn't have it; she just kept going on and on with her side until she finally convinced him."

"Can't say I'm surprised at that. Then what happened?"

"Then they got into an awful argument about what to do with me."

"And you heard that, too?"

"Yep, all of it. My mom thought they should help me be the person I was born to be, but my dad said she was putting too much into it, that I was just a sensitive child and they should leave it at that. Mom said no, it was more than being sensitive. Dad said if they let it be more, if they encouraged it, sooner or later I'd be blamed for the things that happened. Either that or people would start thinking I was a freak. He said it was best to ignore the whole thing, let me grow up like a normal kid. Then Mom asked who was he to decide what was normal? Then he said it was their job to protect me and that's what they needed to do. They fought and fought and never did come together. Finally, they walked away from the table, and Dad slept on the couch that night. For weeks after that, they hardly spoke." CeeGee stopped and looked out the window again, her face tight and red. "The whole thing was my fault."

"Your fault? Again? How do you figure this was all your fault?"

"Well, can't you see? I didn't help anyone with my Knowings, and then I ruined my parent's marriage, really my whole family, because of it."

"Celia Gene, that is not at all what I take from this story you've been telling me."

Just then, the ferry worker waved them onto the boat. CeeGee pushed her glasses up on her nose, crossed her arms over her chest and glared at him.

As Mr. Tindale started the car he said, "All right, child, don't get all stubborn. Let me get on the boat and then you can tell me what happened after your parents had this big fight."

Once they boarded the ferry and parked the car, CeeGee uncrossed her arms and eyed Mr. Tindale suspiciously. He gave her a kind nod, and she went on. "Okay, after they fought, I played everything they said over and over in my mind. I was trying to decide who was right and it was all I could think of for days and days and days. I think I'm more like my dad than my mom, so in the end I went with his side. It wasn't hard, really, because no one needed to blame me for anything, I already blamed myself. And, for sure, I thought I was a freak.

"I decided I would be what he wanted—a nice, normal kid. I knew the only way I could do that was to shut out the light forever. So, I figured out how to keep everything outside of myself, and not let anything come in. Not feelings, not radio signals, not light and, for sure, not Knowings. When school started again, I worked to get good grades, so my parents wouldn't get called back in. And I did just enough in class to make it look like I was interested. I spent time in the library and read a lot of books, so no one would bother with me. I just got, real… real… alone."

"Did your parents try to talk to you or anything?"

"For a while they did, they kept trying to get me to have these big heart-to-heart talks with them, but I'd never talk about the Knowings, so they finally gave up. I acted pretty normal at home, you know, scrapping with Danny and Davey, doing my chores, reading my books." Then CeeGee smiled softly and added, "And after a while they got back close to each other—I don't think either one of them is very good at staying mad, thank goodness. So, things finally settled down, but only because I'd quit letting the light come in."

"And that's how you've been living until that day in my garden?" CeeGee nodded and Mr. Tindale shook his head back at her. "Celia Gene, you have surely been through a trying time. And this story you've been telling me, well, it hurts my heart to hear it. I don't know what it feels like to have a gift like you do, but I do know from living my own long life that you and your Knowings were not the cause of everything that happened. People die at all ages and for all kinds of reasons—school can be hard, parents fight, children have struggles, sometimes people feel like they don't fit in." He paused and started the engine. "Child, we're here at the dock, and I think I have the story. I believe you are telling me the truth about your Knowings and I aim to help you somehow, I truly do. But I got to sort some things out, and I need time for myself to think things through. I got to figure out the difference between what has been and what could be."

The ferry director waved them off the boat.

CeeGee studied Mr. Tindale's face. She felt scared that he would get mad or give up before he could help her. What if he died? She wanted to grab him, make him keep talking. She wanted him to look at her. He didn't look upset or lost, but he was off somewhere in his own thoughts and she didn't think she could reach him wherever he was.

He stopped at Southport's only stoplight, looked at her and said, "All right, let's get you on home now, child. If you give me a night to think, I figure I'll be ready to see you for breakfast in the mornin'.'"

CeeGee felt a small whoosh of relief, but only a small one. Tomorrow, a whole other day. Once they got to his house, he stopped before he pulled into the garage. CeeGee started to get out of the car, but Mr. Tindale reached out and touched her arm. "Let's sit here just one more moment," he said. He turned and looked at her seriously. "Celia Gene, I believe what you've been telling me. And to me it means you are special, not cursed. I know it doesn't feel like a gift to you, but I think it is."

"You're right, it doesn't feel like a gift to me at all."

"And you understand, don't you, that gifts are for others, not for ourselves."

"Yes, like birthday presents. I know that."

"Right, so let's do a test, let's find out if it's just your gift. I want you to try something before you come see me tomorrow."

"I will, Mr. Tindale, I'll do anything. What do you want me to do?"

"I want you to get a Knowing on yourself."

"What?" She cocked her head to one side and pushed her glasses up on her nose. "I don't understand."

"Well, what I'm thinking is, if these Knowings are all about you, the way you been saying, that you made things happen, that you should have warned people, that you ruined your parents—that when it comes to the Knowings it's all about you. If all that's so, then why didn't you know your own future? Like where you were headed in school, or that your parents would get called in, and that your momma would figure everything out. Why didn't you know that your parents would fight, and then get over it, and get back to loving each other same as they always had. I'm wondering, why didn't you ever have a Knowing on yourself? So, I want you to see if you can."

"I never thought of it that way."

Well, then, I'd like you to think of it that way. Can you do that?"

"Yes, sir, I'll try."

"All right then, let's gather up our things, and I'll look forward to seein' you in the morning."

CeeGee took his package of fabric, got out of the car and took it around to the porch and set it on the rocker. Mr. Tindale pulled his car into the garage and parked it, then came hobbling around to the front where CeeGee was waiting for him with her bicycle. They walked together to the driveway and CeeGee turned away from him and started to get on her bike.

"Wait a moment, one last thing," Mr. Tindale said. CeeGee turned back to him with tears streaming down her face. She didn't want him to see her crying like this. He smiled at her softly, reached out and squeezed her shoulder, "You got work to do, child, but I want you to know I aim to help you like I promised."

"You will, you really promise?"

"I really promise. And I want to thank you for going shopping with me and helping me pick out that nice satin. That was a generous thing to do. Now you best get on home." He waved his hand at her, "Run on now. You study on it serious like, and I'll be seein' you for breakfast tomorrow."

She turned away, got on her bike and began to ride, feeling as bad as she did the day she told Mr. Tindale he was going to die. After all her talking, and his listening, she still didn't understand one single thing. CeeGee didn't feel like she could go home yet. She rode her bike away from Mr. Tindale's and headed to the marsh, parking by the box at the entry that held the guides. She didn't need a guide to the marsh, she needed a guide to herself. She walked down the path and onto the boardwalk and kept going until she got to the bench in the middle.

She sat, surrounded by the marsh. Here in the calm, the only sounds were the slap of the surge against the mossy bank, the singing of the birds, and the squish of turtles as they foraged in the grass. She leaned back and tried to let the marsh melody fill her, join her to the world and make her one with it, instead of the other thing, the freak, the outsider she always felt herself to be.

Mr. Tindale's words kept coming back to her. Did she have a gift, instead of a curse? Was it really all about the others? And was there a way she could learn to help, to give her gift instead of feeling punished by it? She looked back through the years and realized she never did get a Knowing on herself. What did that mean? These thoughts looped around in her head until she decided she would do what Mr. Tindale asked. She would try and make a Knowing come. Maybe she could find out what *her* future was going to be.

She stood up and looked out across the marsh waters. Then she raised her arms up high and looked to the sky like an old-timey preacher would do. No light. She made fists and shook them up at the sky a few times. Nothing. She put her arms down to her sides and squatted low, squeezed her eyes shut, waited a while, then peeked up, hoping to catch a glimpse of the light. Nothing. She stomped her feet and tried the entire procedure again three or four more times. Nothing, nothing, nothing. Except the tourists down at the end of the boardwalk turned to stare at her strangely. As strangely as she felt.

She gave up, went back to the entry, got on her bike and rode home. She climbed the stairs from the carport to the kitchen, and with each step made herself turn back into that normal child, the one who had no worries and caused no trouble. She was so, so tired.

Chapter Seven

The next morning, CeeGee rode her bike to Mr. Tindale's house, but he wasn't on the front porch where he belonged. This scared her at first—what if he had gone and died on her after all? She banged on the screen door and breathed a sigh of relief when she heard him call her in. She found him standing at the kitchen stove.

"Hello, child. Thought you might be getting here early and would want a bite to eat." CeeGee could hear the kindness in his voice and started to tear up again. "Sit down at the table. I'm making some breakfast for us like I promised."

Mr. Tindale had already set two places with bowls, big spoons and napkins, and he'd put a pitcher of milk, a butter dish, raisins, brown sugar and salt in the middle of the table. CeeGee wiped her eyes and sank into a chair. As she looked at the table setting, the thought occurred to her that Mr. Tindale was a lot like her mom. Whenever there was something really hard to talk about, they both put food in front of her. It sure did serve to make things easier. "What are you making?" she asked.

"Skillet oatmeal. It'll put some meat on your bones and get you ready to sort things out with me." He turned around and gave her a good morning smile and a nod. "Now, watch how I do this, child. I'm fixin' to make the best oatmeal under the sun, not all pasty and gooey like most folks make it. Skillet oatmeal has a nice nutty texture and holds up to whatever you want to put on top of it." Mr. Tindale turned the heat on his gas range up to high, then used a measuring cup to pour a couple of inches of water into an old cast iron skillet like the one CeeGee's grandmother had handed down to her mother. When the water started to boil, he slowly sprinkled oatmeal over the top. "The trick," he explained, "is to add just enough oatmeal to the water so's it doesn't sink down anymore. That's how you know you got the right amount. Since the oatmeal is all spread out in a wide, shallow pan, it cooks in a hurry. You only want to be stirring till it soaks up the boiling water and the oatmeal looks like a bubbling tar pit. Then it's done."

"What's a bubbling tar pit?"

"Like it sounds, a big old pool of boiling, melted tar."

"That doesn't sound too appetizing."

"Celia Gene, just hush up and trust me on this." He brought the skillet over, spooned half the oatmeal into her bowl, the other half in his, and sat down.

It looked so good and CeeGee was so hungry she forgot all about the tar pit, but she did remember to put her napkin in her lap. She started to add the extras to her oatmeal.

Mr. Tindale said, "You want to bury a nice big pat of butter right in the middle of the hot oatmeal."

CeeGee buried the butter, then added milk, brown sugar and raisins. "What's the salt for?"

"A fine bowl of oatmeal requires just a dash of salt to bring out the flavor." CeeGee salted her oatmeal and Mr. Tindale sat back and waited for her to take her first bite. "Well?"

"This is good, Mr. Tindale, this is real good. I'm going to tell my momma about this."

"You ought to get up early one morning and fix it for your momma. That's what you ought to do."

"That's a good idea. I'll do that." They settled into eating and the kitchen got quiet, so all of CeeGee's bad feelings had time to come back.

Mr. Tindale reached out and patted her hand. "Don't worry, child, we're here to make things better, not worse. You trust me on that?"

"Yes, sir, I guess so." Once again, she had the feeling he had read her mind.

"So, second question. Did you get that Knowing on yourself?"

"No, sir, I didn't. I tried and tried at the marsh yesterday, but I never did."

"So, you wonder why that might be?"

All the fear and frustration CeeGee had felt for so long came pouring out of her. "Here's what I wonder. I wonder—why me? Why'd I have to have this thing? It's never done me, or anyone, any good at all. It's just bad news."

"Just stay calm, missy. We're going to get this all sorted out. Let's sum it all up." He pointed at the air with his spoon like a music conductor. "First off, far as you're concerned, the only good thing about your gift was the time you saved your momma from getting hit by a baseball, right?" CeeGee thought for a second, then nodded. "But you think there's a lot of bad things, like how your Knowings were about hard times for folks, or even folks passing on. Plus, you got your parents and your teachers all riled up. That right, too?" CeeGee nodded again. "And even though, the way you been seeing it, the gift is all about you—it's a true thing you never got a single Knowing about your own future, even when you tried. Right again?"

CeeGee kept quiet and just nodded.

"Does this tell you anything?" Mr. Tindale asked, setting down the spoon and folding his arms across his chest.

"It tells me that having this gift is a real pain."

"I'd say, contrary to what you been thinking, it tells you this gift ain't for you."

"You keep saying that, but I don't get how it can be my gift and not be for me."

"If it's for you, why can't you get a Knowing on yourself? Explain that to me."

"I can't explain that, but it's still my gift," CeeGee insisted.

"It ain't."

"Is too."

"Ain't."

"Is."

"Well, Miss Williamson, if you ask me, your stubborn thinking is what's made you so miserable and kept things from turning out right."

"Wait a minute!" She pointed at him accusingly. "What about your light?"

"What light?"

"It's a rainbow around your head. I saw it when I was little, and I saw it again in front of the Triple S the other day."

"You're sayin' I have a rainbow around my head?"

"Yes, you do. I can see it."

"You sure? I never knew that." Mr. Tindale reached up and touched the top of his head like he was adjusting a crown and smiled.

"So, do you have a gift from your light? Have you made things okay with it?"

"I don't have the slightest idea, Celia Gene. I mean, I know I've always been real sensitive to how other people might be feeling, like your dad said about you. But I never knew I had a light. It's nice rainbow colors, you say?"

"Yes, and that doesn't answer my question."

He quit smiling and looked at her seriously. "Now you listen, young lady, because I am talking to you straight. I am nothing like you, Celia Gene. I don't know things the way you do, never have. I'm happy to hear you say I have just a little light of my own because it makes me think I might be able to help you through this." He looked over at her, then said slow and serious, "But, in order for me to help, you have to hear what I'm saying, so let's quit trying to change the subject and get back to you, your gift, your Knowings."

"All right, I'm listening." He looked at her suspiciously. "I am," CeeGee said.

"All right then, here's what I have to say to you. You haven't been *given* a gift, child. You have a gift to *give*. It's not for you, it's for the others."

There was a long silence as CeeGee sat still, trying to absorb Mr. Tindale's meaning. "I don't get it," she said finally.

"I'd say you're no different than anyone else. The way I see things, we each got the same job in this life. Our job here on earth is to figure out our gifts and learn how to give 'em."

CeeGee got quiet while the wisdom of Mr. Tindale's words gradually sank in. After a while, she spoke up, "I want to help people with my gift, I do. But no matter what I want, or how hard I try, my Knowings bring nothing but trouble."

"Maybe that's because you haven't grabbed on to the other piece. It's that we need to give our gifts, each of us, with a kind and generous heart. For the benefit of others."

"So, my heart has not been kind?"

"I think you've been too troubled and frightened by your gift and the things you've known to think about the others. But you just told me, that's what you really wanted. And now, together, I think we can figure out how you can have that kind and generous heart every time."

CeeGee slowly folded her napkin. She ran her fingers along the creases the way her mother would do and set it on the table. She finally looked up at him. "I feel terrible, Mr. Tindale. After listening to you, I feel like I've been cursing at God or something."

"At first you were too young to understand this at all, Celia Gene. Now it's time for you to start thinking less about yourself and more about the folks who might need to hear what you have to say. Seems to me, at the heart of it, you got a chance to tell people what direction they're headed. Then maybe some of 'em have a chance to change direction, if they want."

CeeGee just shook her head.

"Girl, what are you, twelve years old?"

"Thirteen—in a week."

"Okay, thirteen. You're just now old enough to make a start at understanding it all. That's why you came to me. So maybe together we can figure out how you can give your gift the way you're supposed to."

"Do you really think we can?"

"Yes, missy, I do. In fact, you already got started by helping Mike Robins get the idea to build my casket. He needed the work and you helped him out without a thought for yourself, far as I can see."

"I did?"

"Yes, you did, and with us workin' together, it'll be more of the same."

"That'd be good, Mr. Tindale. That'd be real good."

Mr. Tindale got up, took their spoons and bowls and hobbled over to the sink.

"There's still some stuff I don't get," CeeGee said as he turned on the faucet and began to wash their bowls.

"Shoot."

"Well, how can I help someone if they're just going to die, like Mr. Jennings and Kenny?"

Mr. Tindale turned and leaned against the kitchen counter. "Well, maybe it's so's you can help the living go on a little better. Take that first time with Mr. Jennings, was he in that parking lot?"

"I think so. Yes, I remember he was there, too."

"But, funny thing, you ran to his wife to say sorry to her, you went to the person who would still be here. Even at four, I'm guessing you knew that the sorrow was hers."

"I did."

"Right. And, let's take Kenny the Paperboy. He had a hard life that boy, barely able to walk and talk. And his momma had a hard job caring for him."

"But she loved Kenny more than anything. It was terrible for her when he died."

"I know it was, and she needed to leave the island after a time to lift her heart. But I heard she's gone back to school. She's gettin' her degree in education and wants to work with young people like Kenny."

"Still, that still doesn't bring Kenny back."

"But, Kenny doesn't have to come back for her to go on. Maybe now she'll do a lot more with her life than caring for just one child. Maybe Kenny's time was full, he was ready and her hard job was done. Maybe you knew and that's why you didn't feel sad when you waved goodbye to Kenny. Now his momma is taking what she learned from Kenny, adding to it and settin' out to help a whole bunch of people—people who really need someone like her. That's not so terrible, is it? Don't you think this could be a good life for her?"

"Yes, it could be." CeeGee thought for a moment. "Okay, but what about when my gift doesn't work?"

"Like when?" Mr. Tindale asked.

"Like with you. I had a Knowing you were gonna die, too. We can see I didn't get that one right."

"But you were right."

CeeGee cleared the rest of the table, took everything to the counter and stood next to him. "In case you hadn't noticed, you're still here."

He looked down at her. "I was a dying man, and I knew the truth of it soon as you said it. That's why it made me so mad. I was killing myself with grief over my dear Maggie May. But, you gave me some good advice, said to get ready, think about what I needed to do in the time left to me. I'm gonna die all right, but I'll leave this here earth with my affairs in order, and not as soon as I might have, thanks to you."

"Still, I was wrong."

"What? Did you have an exact date in mind? Am I supposed to die on your particular schedule? Like I said earlier, Celia Gene, it ain't about you being wrong or right. Besides, sometimes things that seem bad at first can turn out to be good in the end."

"Yeah? Name one." CeeGee took the dishtowel off the hook and began drying their breakfast bowls.

Mr. Tindale finished rinsing out the skillet, using hot water but no soap, exactly like her mother. He put it on the counter to air dry, took the dishtowel out of her hands, dried his own and turned away from the sink. "Here, let's sit back down." He waited for her to get settled, then he said, "First off, I think you have to accept that this gift is bigger than you are, and you're not ever going to understand every single thing about it. You just have to figure out what you can, and do your best to honor that."

CeeGee shook her head and brushed the spilled salt off the tabletop. Mr. Tindale waited until she was done before he went on. "Let's think of it this way. Say you're sitting beside a tide pool, watching the hermit crabs scurrying around. You know that tiny little pool is their whole world, right?"

"Okay, I've done that." CeeGee said, looking back up at him.

"Good. So, you're watching these busy little critters in their tiny world. Then you look out to the sea, and there is the tide roiling, about to come in again, ready to flood that tiny pool. And you know a few hours later the tide will go back out and the crabs will be high and dry. So, you have a much bigger view of the world than those little crabs. Right?"

"Yeah, that'd be right."

"So, even beyond the tide, there's the whole Gulf of Mexico splayed out in front of you," Mr. Tindale spread his arms out wide, "and the wide-open Texas sky above. You can see the birds on the shore and the grassy dunes behind. And, there's the whole star-filled universe beyond that," he swept his hands toward the heavens, "and even more that we don't know about yet. So, in a way, your world is just as small as that little hermit crab. Both you and that creature are a tiny part of this whole big thing, way bigger than you can know."

"You're making my head hurt."

"I'm just saying that even though you have this big gift, you still can't see the *how* of everything, or know the *why* of everything. Not any more than a tiny crab in a tide pool."

"Hey, wait a second." Suddenly CeeGee sat up straight and pointed her finger at Mr. Tindale's chest. "I remember that tide pool stuff. It's from that John Steinbeck book, *Cannery Row*. Right?"

"How'd you know that?"

"Because my mom gave it to me and I read it along with her English class."

"Well then, you ought to get what I'm talking about," he said.

"I do get it," CeeGee protested. "I mean I didn't then, exactly, but I do now. Kinda."

"You get a lot more than you think, Celia Gene. You know about the Golden Rule, don't you? That we're supposed to treat others the way we'd like to be treated. That's really all you need to do. Just follow the Golden Rule and you'll be fine."

They sat in silence while CeeGee tried to put the jigsaw pieces of all Mr. Tindale had said into a picture she could see and understand. Finally, she said, "I think what you're saying about the

Golden Rule goes along with what my mom always taught me and the twins. She says we should never try to make ourselves feel big by making others feel small."

"That's exactly what I'm saying. When you need to give somebody a Knowing, you want to think about how you'd want to be told. You want to consider their feelings and their privacy."

"That sounds pretty hard."

"Did you think giving your gift the right way was going to be easy, child?"

"Guess not." CeeGee turned her face away so Mr. Tindale wouldn't see her struggling not to cry—again.

Mr. Tindale reached out and squeezed her shoulder. "I know you got a big job in front of you, Celia Gene. But you've been picked out specially to do it, and I have to figure that was for a reason. So, don't you worry none, you'll be fine, just fine."

"You promise you'll be here to help me?"

"I'm certain of it, long as you need me."

CeeGee couldn't help herself. She leaned over, put her arms around his neck and cried out of fear and relief and hope.

"There, there now," Mr. Tindale said as he patted her back. "We're about to set off on a grand adventure, Celia Gene. That's what we're about to do."

Chapter Eight

Off the seaward coast of Magdalena Island, there are three long sandbars running parallel to the shore. The first is easy to see because the sandbar is close in and rises above the surface with each set of receding waves. The second is dimmer, a band of pale tan in the gray-green water, a long stone's throw from the bank. The third is about the length of a football field offshore. It's just a dim line and can only be seen by someone who knows what they're looking for.

Getting to the third sandbar to go fishing is an exhausting struggle of splashing and kicking through shallow, choppy waves, while holding a baited fishing rod up high out of the water. Then climbing through soft sand to the top, standing in knee-deep, swirling water and casting against the wind into the surf. But it's worth it because there, on the third sandbar, is the best fishing on the entire Gulf Coast, or so CeeGee had always been told. Whether or not it was actually true didn't really matter to her, because as soon as she was old enough to swim, the third sandbar was CeeGee's very most favorite place in all the world—the place where she had her dad all to herself.

On her birthday, June 10th, CeeGee's father stood on top of the third sandbar, tall as a statue with the wind blowing his sandy hair into his eyes, squinting to find the swirls and eddies where the best fish might be. CeeGee stood tall and proud next to him, also squinting as she searched, since both of them had left their glasses on a towel back at the beach.

CeeGee waited for her father to point, like he always did, and say, "There's the spot. See over there—where it's scooped out? There's fish feeding in there, no doubt about it." He would move to the spot and CeeGee would follow and wait for her instructions. "We'll cast from here, Celia Gene. Watch out for the wind. Get on over to the side of it, keep your pole up high now, cast it short and low so your line doesn't blow back in."

The wind swirling around them, the waves breaking on the shore in the distance and the familiar sound of her father's voice— all of this was woven together inside of her like the melody of a familiar lullaby or the chapters of a favorite storybook. She'd heard it just the same for years. It was the sound of her dad saying, 'I love you,' the best way he knew how.

In between casts, CeeGee looked back to the shore at Danny and Davey flinging their skim boards into the edge of the surf and running after them to jump on and take a ride. They rode like lightening, fell off the boards into the shallow surf, splashed each other, then pushed each other out of the way to be first for the next ride. Again and again and again. She could hear their shouts and laughter all the way out to the third sandbar. From this distance she could see their magical connection as they touched, danced, knitted themselves together all through the day, as they always had. They needed no one, they were bookends, a complete set.

Her gaze shifted to her mother, leaning back against a low beach chair, a big straw hat shielding her red hair and pale skin from the sun. Bobbie slowly turned the pages of the book she held, glancing up occasionally to make sure the twins weren't getting into trouble. As CeeGee watched her, Bobbie turned to look out to the sandbar, shielding her eyes and waving. CeeGee waved back, wondering, not for the first time, how did she know I was looking at her? How does she know?

By afternoon, CeeGee had caught three good-sized redfish and her Dad two, so they had enough to make up dinner for the whole family. They got into the station wagon, drove back to town and parked at Pelican's Roost. Danny and Davey carried the ice chest full of redfish into the restaurant and the hostess sent the cook out to greet them, so each person in the family got to order how they'd like their fish prepared. CeeGee ordered pan fried with butter and lemon and her parents wanted a fancy Redfish Amandine. Danny and Davey insisted on ruining a perfect meal of fresh-caught fish by ordering theirs glopped up in corn meal and deep fried.

After they finished their dinner, the waiter brought a cake with thirteen candles to the table, which CeeGee blew out in one try. "Good, sis! You got the wish!" Davey said.

Danny reached over and slapped her shoulder. "What'd you wish for? Boobs?"

"Enough." Carl admonished.

Bobbie leaned down and got her purse, opened it, took out a tiny gift-wrapped present and handed it across the table to CeeGee. Inside was CeeGee's very first real gold necklace, a tiny sand dollar hanging on a delicate chain. It had a note in the package that said, 'Happy Birthday to our Celia Gene on your big day. You will always be our light and our love. From Mom and Dad'. Bobbie got up and walked around the table to fasten it for her, then kissed the top of her head.

Her dad said, "Thirteen years old, Celia Gene, big year. Now you've also become a dreaded teenager." He looked at the twins and grimaced.

"Dad," Danny said, "we are *fine* boys. Mom said so, I heard her tell her friends!"

Carl replied, "There is no such thing as fine fifteen-year-old boys, especially when they come in two's."

"Now, Carl," Bobbie squeezed his arm.

Then, to CeeGee's surprise, Danny and Davey actually gave her a present, too—a little shell-covered jewelry box from a tacky store to keep her necklace in. Theirs didn't have a note, but still, it was nice.

Everything was perfect. It was her birthday, school was out for the summer and she got all A's—again. She went fishing with her dad, caught three redfish and now she had a grownup necklace. CeeGee was starting to believe that maybe Mr. Tindale was right, maybe something new had begun, something that would be a grand adventure. Maybe with all these good feelings she could have her Knowings the way he said—a Knowing that would help someone, a Knowing that would be a gift for others.

The next day, Mr. Tindale asked CeeGee to come over. When she arrived, he was sitting in his rocker with a birthday present in his lap, tied up with a sloppy bow, the gift wrap patched with tape here and there. "Not so good at wrapping presents," Mr. Tindale said as she came up the steps.

He handed her the box, which was so big she had to sit down on the porch to open it. Inside was a new bicycle basket with a horn attached to the outside. When CeeGee squeezed the horn, the bleat sounded like the kind a clown would make in a rodeo. "Oh, Mr. Tindale, this is so nice, and the basket is so big!"

"Well, child, you keep on hauling these library books around, so I thought you might need a little more space. And just in case someone gets in your way, you can tell 'em what for with that there horn."

"I love it. I love both of them."

"I checked in with Mike and he says he can put it on your bike, easy as pie. So, when he's done with the casket and ready for us to put in the lining, we can take your bike over there in my trunk."

☆☆☆☆

It seemed like Mike would never call. They didn't want to pester him, but they couldn't wait to see what he would build for Mr. Tindale's final resting place. Weeks went by with the bicycle basket and horn sitting on top of the counter in Mr. Tindale's garage.

Finally, Mike called. He told Mr. Tindale he was ready for them to come on over and put the satin lining in the new casket. Mr. Tindale asked CeeGee to come by his house first and they would drive over together. They loaded up the car with CeeGee's bike and the bicycle basket and horn and drove to Mike's house. Mike was waiting for them in the carport, excited to show Mr. Tindale the casket, but also his other surprise.

"You know," Mike said, "I felt bad taking that extra cash from you, sir. But since you held firm, I wanted to do something with the money that was worth your kindness. So here it is, thanks to you." He waved his arm around the carport, then started the tour. "So, I made this here plywood wall across the back of the carport, so's I can put my tools up nice and neat. And I added this workbench."

Mike beamed with pride. The wooden wall he had built covered the whole back end of his carport and the workbench stretched the whole length of the wall. The bench was high, so he could work standing up, or at a high stool, which he had tucked under the bench. He'd put nails and hooks on the wall behind the bench to hang up all his tools. He was so tidy and orderly that he even made an outline for each tool, so he knew just where to put them back when he was done using them.

"Now, at the end of the day," he motioned them away from the workbench and into the center of the carport. "I can close off the whole space with these here big wooden doors." He walked over to one door, released the latch and began to pull it closed, then he moved the door back to open. "And see here, when they're open they make the carport shady on the sides, but when I swing them together," he demonstrated as he spoke, "I can lock the place off with a padlock, so's all my tools are safe."

There was so little crime in Southport most people didn't even lock their houses, but Mike's tools were all that stood between feeding his family and going hungry, so he decided to be more cautious than most. Mike crossed his arms, looked at his doors, then grinned at CeeGee and Mr. Tindale.

Once they were done with the tour, and CeeGee and Mr. Tindale had praised Mike for his design skills and tidiness, Mike took them over to the middle of the carport where something big was sitting on top of two sawhorses. He pulled off a tarp and there was Mr. Tindale's new casket. Mike told them he set it up on the sawhorses to make it easier for them to do their work. He'd also set up a folding worktable and laid out an array of tools nice and neat. "So, here's all the tools we need," Mike said as he pointed to each item, "tape measures, scissors, glue guns, staplers and these here fancy little bronze thumbtacks." He'd cut the quilt padding and satin to fit and made up lengths of piping for them to use around the edges. In fact, he'd done so much work ahead of time a person might think that Mike was the one who actually lined the casket, but he would never take credit, and CeeGee and Mr. Tindale would never admit to that.

The casket was as beautiful as Mr. Tindale hoped it would be. It was oak, like he wanted, and the finish wasn't shiny at all, but satiny like the blue lining. CeeGee said the wood seemed to glow from the inside out and Mike told her that was because he waxed it by hand, over and over, until he got it to look that way. It had only one lid, not two like some caskets because Mr. Tindale thought having two lids was ridiculous. "Why would anyone go out and spend good money on a brand new burial suit if folks are only going to see you in half of it?"

Mike made the casket rounded on top. He explained that he did this by cutting long pieces of oak with the sides angled just so, then glued them together and sanded them off so perfectly you could barely see the joints. There was simple wood beading around the edge of the lid, bronze handles at each end and long rails down the sides. Mike explained to CeeGee that the long rails down the sides of the casket were for people called 'pallbearers' to carry the casket from the funeral service to the graveside. Mike knew how CeeGee liked new words, so he'd looked up pallbearer for her in the encyclopedia. He said the word came from a heavy cloth that was draped over a coffin called the 'pall'. The term "pallbearer" is the person who bears the coffin that is covered by the pall. CeeGee liked it. The word had a nice sound to it, and she thought it a kindness on such a day to gather the folks closest to the departed to perform this service.

Before they got started, Mr. Tindale asked Mike if he'd do one more thing. He opened the trunk to show him the bike and the new basket and horn. Mike lifted it all out, and in what seemed like a minute, took off CeeGee's old basket, hooked up the new one and blasted the horn a few times to the tune of happy birthday. CeeGee thanked him and said, "Say, Mike, could one of your kids use the basket you took off?"

"Sure, Celia Gene, why that's a fine idea," Mike said. "Thanks for thinkin' of that," he said as he set the basket on his workbench.

Since it was so still and hot in the carport, Mike had also set up a huge fan back in the corner that stood on a pedestal as tall as a man and put out a wind so strong CeeGee had to pull her hair back in a rubber band to keep it from blowing into the glue. Mike pointed up to the roof of the carport. "If I ever get a little money ahead, I'm going to put me up a big-ass ceiling fan. Oh, sorry for cussin' in front of Celia Gene here."

Mr. Tindale patted his shoulder and said, "Mike, this beautiful casket makes a man rest easier about the fact of dyin'. Seems a shame to put it in the ground, though." He ran his hand across the top of it a few times, like he was stroking Spunk the cat, then shook out his shoulders and turned to look at Mike and CeeGee. "Now, let's put in that baby blue satin lining and finish her off," he said grinning.

They went to work, folding the corners just so, tacking in the lining and gluing the piping on carefully so none of the glue would leak out and stain the satin. Just as they were finishing up, the light came into CeeGee with a warm and soft feeling. Without even needing to talk to Mr. Tindale, she knew just what to say about this Knowing because, even though this one had a sad part, it connected the dots from her first Knowing on Mike and shot it all into the future like a shining star.

She stood back and put her hands on her hips, "Mike, this is just about the most beautiful thing I've ever seen. I think you ought to take it over to Sandwith Brothers' Funeral Home and show it off to them."

Mr. Tindale looked over at her and said, "Why, that's a fine idea, Celia Gene. I bet seeing the work Mike has done here, why those fellas would get a whole new idea of what a proper casket should look like."

Mike was proud of his work and did just that. The Sandwith brothers were so impressed they ordered five more caskets, so they'd have them ready made for customers. In the meantime, they asked for permission to put Mr. Tindale's casket on display. They also asked Mike to make up samples of all the different kinds of woods he could use because they figured some people would want custom, and they didn't think everyone would want oak.

They told Mike they sold caskets all up and down the Texas Coastal Bend, so they were sure he'd get more orders. They worked out prices so Mike would make a profit and they would too. Then they did some advertising, and in no time at all, Mike started getting those custom orders. It turned out Mr. Tindale wasn't the only person in Texas who made their plans in advance and wanted to be laid to rest in a fine, handmade wooden casket. CeeGee wondered if maybe, when Mike decided to build that nice home workshop, he'd had a little Knowing of his own.

Later, CeeGee and Mr. Tindale talked about her Knowing. She told him it was like the next chapter of a story. First, she knew Mike was going to be able to work on his own, and now she knew that Mike's lifelong dream about making custom furniture for a living was finally going to come true, only he'd be making caskets instead of coffee tables. He was going to be busy in his workshop, and it was a good thing that he was all set to go. In a way, being out of work for a time, and the little bit of money Mr. Tindale paid him, had given him the time and space to get ready for the next chapter of his life. But then she told him the rest of the Knowing, the third chapter, which was sad for Mike Robins and his children. It was another death—Mrs. Robins was not going to recover from her illness.

Mr. Tindale said, "All right, child. Here is our first chance to do what we planned. We need to take this last part of your Knowing, while sad, and make it into a chance for us to be kind and generous to those who have to carry on." After they talked it through, CeeGee understood that even though her Knowing was about the death of Mrs. Robins, her task, along with Mr. Tindale, was to help Mike and his kids get through it a little better. They began to look for ways they could help ease the way for this family in the hard times ahead.

First off, Mr. Tindale invited Mike over to get his final payment and they set it up so that CeeGee would introduce him to Mr. Tindale's housekeeper, Rosa Leon. Rosa was known all over the island for being able to do anything to make the inside of a house shine and sparkle. Mr. Tindale had hired her to keep up his house because he was sick of feeling like a failure compared to Maggie May. Besides, he figured he was going to be so busy helping CeeGee with her Knowings he couldn't be spending his time cleaning house every day.

CeeGee took Mike all around to show him how spic and span the house was, then pulled him aside. "So, Mike, now that you've got some steady work coming in, and especially since your wife is still so sick, I was thinking, maybe you'd want to hire Rosa, too. She only comes here in the mornings, so she could go over to your place in the afternoons. That way she'd be there when the kids got home from school. She could help with their studies and get dinner started. I'm only asking because Rosa told me she could use more work to take care of her family, and I thought you'd understand, having been in that position yourself. When you needed work, I mean."

"I don't know, Miss Celia Gene," Mike said, shaking his head. "I been high and dry for a while. Maybe I'd best save my pennies right now."

Mr. Tindale piped in, "Now, Mike, with the Sandwith Brothers in your corner, and these orders you got, I truly believe you can trust the future, far as your business is concerned. Besides, Rosa could help ease the strain on your wife, give her time to enjoy her family while she's feeling so poorly. Help you out, too, since you'll be needing all your time to get your casket orders finished and catch up on your finances."

Mike agreed to interview Rosa and invited her over to meet Mrs. Robins. When they decided to hire her, Mrs. Robins was so relieved and thankful she cried for three days.

Once that was settled, CeeGee and Mr. Tindale suggested that the Robins invite Rosa's husband, Juan, to come look at the garden. Juan Leon could do all the things outside the house that Rosa could do on the inside, and he was just as perfect. Mrs. Robins, leaning on Mike's arm, walked around the yard as Juan told them how he could fix things up and make everything tidy and nice. He said it wouldn't take much to get the garden in shape, just some care and attention for the season. The next day, Mike got two more casket orders from the Sandwith Brothers and he and Mrs. Robins decided they better hire Juan, too.

Juan set straight to work on Mrs. Robins' vegetable garden, which was as full of weeds as Mr. Tindale's flower garden had been. CeeGee and Mrs. Robins sat side by side on lawn chairs under a sun umbrella and fanned themselves as they watched Juan prepare the garden for summer planting. Mrs. Robins knew that when the high summer heat came her family could harvest the cucumbers and cantaloupes, peas and sweet potatoes, and best of all, the home-grown okra.

CeeGee knew that Mrs. Robins would no longer be with her family on that harvest day.

Chapter Nine

After watching Juan work for a few hours, CeeGee left the Robins' house and got on her bike with mixed-up feelings. It was hard keeping her balance between the nice, happy side of her Knowing about the Robins family and the truly sad side. She didn't feel like going home and trying to act all normal for her family, so she kept pedaling, riding up and down the old familiar sandy streets of Southport, not paying any attention to where she was going. While she rode, she thought about all the things she and Mr. Tindale had been talking about. She was beginning to understand a few things, but there was still way too much she didn't understand at all. She felt part way good about her gift now, but not all the way good. She knew Mike Robins was going to be able to take care of his family, and she knew that Rosa and Juan would help out with the house and the kids, and she knew she had helped to make that happen. But she also knew that nothing she could say or do would make Mrs. Robins well again. It was heavy, this last part.

After she'd been riding for so long her legs ached, she looked up at a street sign to see where she was. Bream Street, it said. This was the neighborhood in Southport where the streets were named after fish, like Amberjack and Drum and Flounder, all laid out in alphabetical order. The houses were simple and small, some needed paint or a fence repaired and there were no gardens that she could see. Then she remembered—Bream was Ronnie Sampson's street.

As soon as she thought of Ronnie, any good thoughts she had flew straight out of her head.

She remembered the day of her Knowing about Ronnie. CeeGee and her mother were in that crosswalk in town, and he came skidding around the corner in his car and nearly hit them. CeeGee felt the awful light enter her and told her mother that Ronnie would get hurt real bad. And then he had his car accident, and now he was in a wheelchair and would never walk again. She hadn't helped Ronnie, not one little bit. She hadn't told him where he was headed, so he had a chance to change direction. Maybe he would have.

She got off her bike and walked it down Bream. She stopped when she saw Ronnie Sampson's wheel chair ramp on the house a few doors down. She wasn't supposed to be around here. Her father said that even though Ronnie couldn't get in the kind of trouble he did before his accident, he was still mean as a snake and she wasn't to go near him. When Carl and the other men in the Southport Town Club tried to help Ronnie to get around by building the ramp for his wheelchair, he never said thank you to anyone, hardly even spoke, and nobody ever saw him away from his house after they got it finished. He dropped out of high school and in time his wild friends quit coming around. It was like Ronnie just stayed home and hid, and CeeGee could feel the dark sorrow coming from his house.

CeeGee kept on walking, pushing her bike forward, figuring she would walk on past his house and go home. But when she got to his driveway she stopped. There was Ronnie, sitting with his back to her in the deep shade of the carport. He had a bulging canvas bag hanging over the back of his wheelchair and a leather holster with a bunch of little slots in the top of it strapped to the side. Ronnie pulled a knife out of one the slots and flung it at a target hanging on the carport wall. More knives were already in the target, clumped around the bull's eye. Ronnie wheeled over, pulled out the knives one by one and put them back in his holster. Then he turned his wheelchair around and saw CeeGee standing at the end of his drive.

"What are you staring at?" he said.

CeeGee took two steps back before she said, "Nothing. I just happened to be riding by, that's all."

"Ain't you never seen a cripple before?"

CeeGee didn't know what to say to that, so she just stayed put.

"You're that Williamson kid."

"Celia Gene."

"What're you doing on my street? You don't live around here."

"Like I said, I was just out riding around."

Ronnie cocked his head to the side, "Out taking a ride on Bream Street?"

"I, I wasn't paying any attention."

"Yeah, well, now that you know where you are, you can leave."

Again, CeeGee stayed put. "You're a pretty good shot."

Ronnie pulled a knife out of his holster and took aim. "Yeah, I am. So, take off, kid."

CeeGee raised a palm to him, "Okay, okay, I was just leaving." She climbed onto her bike and rode to the corner, but then she felt a tug. She stopped and laid her bike down, turned and started to walk back toward his house. She needed to talk to Ronnie Sampson. As she walked, she felt the light begin to warm her. She stepped into the shade of a scraggly longleaf pine and stayed real still until the Knowing flooded into her. This one wasn't sad like the Knowing about Mrs. Robins, not at all. This one had a real nice feeling, like watching a happy movie.

In her Knowing she saw Ronnie, still in his wheelchair, but not looking angry and surly like he did now. He was handsome and fit. He was in some kind of work shop. Not a homemade one, like Mike Robins', but a fancy one in a big room with a lot of other people, maybe fifteen or twenty. Each person had a wooden work counter with bright lights over it. Ronnie had his own counter, set at just the right height for his wheelchair, and he was drawing. There were more drawings pinned up on the wall next to him. There was a narrow, raised shelf at the back of his counter with holes cut out for all his knives. CeeGee recognized those knives. There were also pots of paints and jars full of brushes lined up neatly along the shelf. The other people in the workshop each had their own special counter, tools and paints, and they were all drawing and making stuff, too. They were talking together and laughing as they worked, like a team or a happy family.

Then the Knowing shifted and she saw Ronnie on a pier, but it wasn't the Southport pier. He was down at the end looking back to shore and there were waves breaking onto the sand. They were big waves, the kind the Magdalena Island got in a storm, only there wasn't any storm. The sky was crisp and clear, and the water was a bright blue-green, not mud-colored like the gulf. She saw people taking pictures of Ronnie with big cameras and he rolled around this way and that, so they could film him at every angle. He held his chin up proud like he belonged exactly where he was.

The Knowing made no sense to CeeGee at all, but one thing was for certain, there was more in store for Ronnie Sampson than sitting in a wheelchair throwing knives at a wall.

CeeGee stepped from behind the tree and walked back down the street to the bottom of Ronnie's drive. He was still there in the shade of the carport, but he wasn't throwing knives anymore, he was whittling on something and concentrating hard. He put one knife back in the holster and pulled out a different one, never taking his eyes off the piece of wood he held in his hands.

"Hey, Ronnie," CeeGee said.

He glanced up briefly and said, "I thought you left," before going back to his work.

CeeGee stood her ground. "What are you making?"

"You didn't hear me?"

"Can I see what you're making?" CeeGee took a tentative step toward him.

Ronnie finally stopped and looked up at her. "What's your first name again, Williamson?"

"CeeGee."

"Why won't you get off my street?"

"I just want to…can I see what you're making?"

"Oh, what the hell." Ronnie held out the piece of wood. "Here."

CeeGee walked up close enough to take it from his hand. She turned it around and around. It was an almost finished model of a bird, with feathers carved into its body and tiny, sharp little eyes. She felt like those eyes were looking right at her. The bird had the most delicate legs and feet and was standing on a little twig base. "My gosh, this looks so real. I've never seen anything like this."

Ronnie cocked his head to the side and looked at her for a long moment, then reached around the back of his wheelchair and lifted off the canvas bag. "Here, I got more."

CeeGee stepped closer and took the bag, knelt on the driveway and laid it down carefully. She reached in and, one by one, pulled out birds. A bird in a nest, a bird with a worm in its beak, a bird with its wings stretched out, getting ready to take off and fly. She looked up at Ronnie, "You did all these?"

"Not much else to do."

"They are so good. They're perfect," CeeGee said as she lifted out even more tiny, delicate, perfect birds.

"Yeah? Well, I got lots of time to practice."

"Have you shown these to anyone?"

"No one's ever asked."

"They look like they should be in a museum or an art gallery. I've never seen anything like this."

"You already said that."

CeeGee arranged the birds in a line on the floor. Each one had a base of some kind, a branch or a nest or a puddle of wood, so they stood up on their tiny legs without tottering or falling over. The sculptures were all the same size and looked to be the same type of bird. She looked up at Ronnie again and said, "I love them."

"Take one," he said.

"What? No, I couldn't do that. They…look at them. They belong together. They should be set out on display somewhere, like a collection." She began to put the birds gently back into the bag. "How do you get your ideas?"

"From this bird hangs around here." He pointed. "Lives up in that tree. Kind of gettin' tired of doin' the same bird over and over, though." He reached out, took the bag from her and hung it back on the wheelchair.

"You want a book?" CeeGee asked.

"For what?"

"For birds. There's this guy named John James Audubon, all he did was draw birds. He tried to draw every single bird in North America. The Southport Library has this whole big book of his drawings. They're amazing."

"How do you know this stuff?"

"I read about him. Want me to bring you the book?"

Ronnie looked at her for a moment, then shrugged and said, "Sure, why not."

"Are you going to be around tomorrow? I can bring it then."

"Yeah, I ain't going anywhere. Bring it whenever you want."

"Okay, okay, I will. See you tomorrow." CeeGee ran to the end of the blocked, grabbed her bike from the dust and rode to the library as fast as she could.

When she got there, shaking and sweaty, CeeGee parked her bike in the rack and opened the big door to the quiet. She went to the bathroom and splashed water on her face. Then she found a table and sat for a minute and tried to quiet her breathing. Finally, she felt calmed down enough to go to the shelf where she knew the John James Audubon book was kept. She pulled it off and carried it back to the table. She opened the book and began turning the pages, trying to think how she would tell Ronnie about these birds. And then she thought about how she wanted to tell him about the bird sanctuary that the town of Southport had built on the marsh a few years back. She bet he had never seen it, living in a wheelchair as long as he had. She remembered when they made the boardwalk, the workers from the city took special care to build gentle ramps so people in wheelchairs could get out on the marsh like everyone else. She kept flipping pages, squirming around in her chair, scooting in closer to the table, pushing back, trying to balance the chair on the back legs. Finally, she noticed a boy on the other side of the table staring at her. "What are you looking at?" she demanded, sounding just like Ronnie Sampson.

"I'm looking at you, wiggling around and making noise and keeping me from getting my reading done."

"Oh, sorry."

The boy looked like he was about her age, with black hair and skin so white it was almost blue. Like CeeGee, he wore glasses, but his had big black frames and the lenses made his eyes look huge and his lashes stand out like lines of ink. "I don't think I've ever seen you before," CeeGee said.

"I'm kind of new. We moved here over Christmas. You're CeeGee Williamson."

"How'd you know that?"

"I just know." He folded his hands and waited a moment before he said, "So do we keep talking or do I get back to my book?"

"What are you reading?"

He closed his book and held it up for her to see. "Right now, I'm reading Shakespeare. *The Merchant of Venice.*"

"For fun? How old are you?"

"I'm eleven, and I just finished seventh grade. I go to a private school on the mainland."

"Shouldn't you be in sixth?"

"We're encouraged to work at our own speed, so I skipped ahead."

"Well, La-Di-Da for you." CeeGee wagged a finger at him.

"I wasn't bragging."

"What's your name anyway?"

He looked irritated. "Elby," he said, "Elby Smith."

"Elby?"

"I'm named after Elbridge Gerry," he sighed and closed his notebook, "one of the signers of the Declaration of Independence. My full name is actually Abraham Elbridge Josiah Oliver Smith."

"Wow, that's a mouthful."

"My parents are very patriotic, so they thought it would be nice to honor our forefathers in naming me. They sifted through all the signers of the Declaration and chose the four most unusual first names for the obvious reason."

"Obvious reason. What?"

"Our last name is Smith," he said, shrugging, as if CeeGee should have figured this out. "My parents' strong sense of democracy didn't extend, however, to giving me a vote on what my own name would be. As soon as I was old enough to talk, I picked out Elbridge as the best of the worst, shortened it to Elby and have never let them call me anything else. So, now you know."

"I never met anyone who picked out their own nickname. I thought only stupid brothers got to do that."

"I don't have any brothers or sisters."

"Lucky you. My real name is Celia Gene. And Gene, G-E-N-E, is a boy's name. I'm named after my mother's mother and my father's father. No one gave me a vote either. On Celia Gene, or on CeeGee."

"So, we have one thing in common, a veto on personal name selection." He snickered and started to go back to his reading.

"So, why do you go to private school on the mainland?" CeeGee asked in a rush.

Elby scooted his chair in closer and seemed to think about the question for a while before he answered, "Because I'm smart," he said quietly. Then he looked CeeGee straight in the eye and added, "Actually, I'm not a little bit smart, I'm a whole lot smart."

CeeGee had a sudden image of this Elby Smith tossed in among the run-of-the-mill students at Southport Junior High. She nodded her head slowly, "Yeah, that makes sense."

Just then, Miss McGuire walked by, put her fingers to her lips and said, "Shhhh!" As usual, she shushed them ten times louder than they were talking.

"So, you want to go to the Triple S and have a float?" CeeGee said. "I get them for free."

"Sure." Elby stood up immediately.

CeeGee checked out the Audubon book, they loaded it in her new bike basket and Elby got on the back rack for the ride. When they got to the Triple S, CeeGee took the book in with her and looked around for an empty booth. There was one all the way in the back and they made their way to it.

Once CeeGee and Elby settled in, Johnny Johanssen came over to take their order, looking like he had crawled out of bed in yesterday's clothes. "Whadda' ya' want?"

"Floats?" CeeGee glanced over at Elby and he nodded. After Johnny shuffled away, she said, "So, what's it like being so smart and all?"

"It's okay." He paused, looked down a second, then went on. "No, that's not true. Actually, most of the time, it's a pain. My parents tell me I'm extremely gifted, which means I have all this responsibility. I'm expected to do better in school than anyone and get into the best college in America. Then I'm supposed to run for president, or become a prize-winning scientist, or do something else really, really important to live up to my great potential. Well, I didn't ask to be born so smart, so I don't see why I have to be so responsible for it."

CeeGee could not believe her ears. Elby was gifted. Not only was he a gifted person, but he thought it was a pain. And Elby's parents were in on his gift, which must make it an even worse pain for him.

"Yeah, I know what you mean," she said.

"How would you know what I mean?"

CeeGee took a breath. In all her life, she had never voluntarily talked about her gift to anyone her own age. Actually, she hardly ever talked to anyone her own age about anything at all. If she opened her mouth and told her secret now, she was afraid her voice would come out squeaky and high and she would fly around the room backwards like a helium-filled balloon and then land on the floor in a stretched-out puddle. "I'm gifted, too," she exhaled in a whisper.

"How so?" Elby whispered back.

CeeGee leaned in closer to him, "I can tell what's going to happen…before it happens."

Elby leaned across the table toward her and cocked his head to one side. "You're kidding me," he said.

Just then, Johnny Johanssen appeared with their order. CeeGee and Elby sat with their eyes locked on each other until Johnny finished sliding their two floats across the table, laid down a couple of napkins and put an iced tea spoon and straw beside each glass.

When Johnny left Elby said, "Prove it."

This guy was smart? "Well, duh, because the things I know are going to happen, *do* happen."

"Like what?"

CeeGee thought of Kenny the Paperboy lying on the street next to his three-wheeler, his head bleeding onto the big rock. She would not tell about Kenny. No, she would not. "Mostly I've known when people were going to die or get hurt in an accident. Different stuff."

"Wow. How many times?"

CeeGee quickly added up the list—baseball through the window, Mrs. Jennings in the parking lot, Kenny Keller, Ronnie Sampson, Mr. Tindale, Mike Robins building the casket, and then getting a new career and Mrs. Robins being too sick to ever get well. Oh, and then Ronnie Sampson, again. A few hadn't happened—yet. "A half dozen or so," she said with a shrug.

"But how…"

Just then her father came up to their booth. Carl was staring at his daughter open-mouthed.

Saved, CeeGee thought. "Hey, Dad," she said.

"Celia Gene." Her father turned and looked Elby up and down.

CeeGee realized her father had never seen her sit with anyone in the Triple S. "Having a good day, Dad?"

"Good enough," he answered, still staring at Elby. He put out his hand, "Hello, young man."

Elby reached over and shook Carl's hand. "Elby Smith, sir."

"Fine, fine," Carl said as he directed his gaze back to his daughter. He reached over to squeeze her shoulder, and CeeGee saw a slight smile cross his face. He turned and left without saying another word.

"That was your Dad?" Elby asked.

CeeGee nodded, the same slight smile crossing her face. "Yeah, he owns this place."

Elby nodded, thought for another moment, then said, "So prove it."

"Prove what?"

"That you know things."

CeeGee looked down at the book, lying between them on the table. "Okay, see this?" She pushed the book toward him, "I have this to take to someone; he's the only person I've ever had two Knowings about. That's what I call them, Knowings." She took a deep breath and began to tell him the whole, long story of Ronnie Sampson. By the time she was finished, she knew for sure this story had not yet ended, and the ending might be a better one than she, or even Ronnie, could have ever dreamed. She sat silently, waiting to hear how Elby would react to her wild tale.

"I think your gift is better than mine," he said.

CeeGee felt one of Ronnie's birds fly right out of her chest.

Elby thought for a moment. "Sounds like your Knowing is saying Ronnie is in California."

"Why do you think that?"

"Because the water is blue, and the waves are big and it's warm and sunny. Sounds to me like California."

"That could be. What about the workshop?"

"Well, if he's in California, then he'd probably be working in the movies. Simple deductive reasoning."

"What's that?"

"It's when you use an if-then proposition. *If* he's in a place with an ocean, it's sunny and nice and he's working at a table making models and drawings, *then* he's probably in California working for the movies. Maybe cartoons? They use drawings and models, right? That part where he's on the pier getting filmed? That sounds like he's an actor."

"How in the heck does a guy sitting in a wheelchair on Magdalena Island get himself all the way to California, land a job with the movies and become an actor?"

"Go to an art school? You said he was good at art with his birds and all. What's the problem?"

"One problem would be that Ronnie never graduated from high school."

"Oh, that would present a problem." Elby thought for a moment. "So, you know anyone who could help him finish high school?"

"Matter of fact, I do." CeeGee said. She immediately began to wonder how she could get her mother to help Ronnie like she had always wanted to, without getting her parents all crazy about her gift again. She'd ask Mr. Tindale. "I'll work on that."

And so, they continued to talk. And they kept on talking—about things CeeGee had never been able to put in words before, not even to Mr. Tindale. They finished their root beer floats, but they didn't leave. They talked about how the world seemed to be a big picture frame and normal people lived inside it, while CeeGee and Elby felt like they watched from the outside. They talked about what it might be like to join everyone and live inside that orderly frame. They questioned where their special gifts came from, and why they came especially to them. They shared their fears that they would never live up to the responsibility of their gifts and wondered what would happen to them if they didn't. Would they be punished and by whom? And if they did live up to their gifts who would they become? Would they always feel alone? They talked and talked, until they both knew they would get into trouble if they didn't get on home.

Chapter Ten

On Sunday morning, CeeGee took the Audubon book to Ronnie Sampson's house, but he wasn't in the carport, and she didn't feel right about knocking on his door. She left the book on a table next to his target where she was sure he'd see it. Then she went over to Mr. Tindale's. She was excited to tell him all about Ronnie and Elby and to see if he could help her push her new Knowing about Ronnie's future in a good direction. He wasn't on the porch, but it didn't scare her. She knew it was getting too hot to be anywhere but inside the house with a fan on high speed blowing straight at you.

She found him sitting at the kitchen table writing on a lined yellow tablet, with a rotating fan set up on the counter beside him. Every time it blew past, a little fringe of his fine, gray hair stood up at attention like one of her brothers' cowlicks. He held up his finger to let her know to be quiet and give him a minute, so she pulled a chair over to the counter, sat down in front of the fan and leaned in close enough for the wind to wiggle the skin on her face as it swept back and forth. Spunk jumped up on her shoulder and CeeGee and Spunk took turns putting their faces right in front of the fan. Actually, only CeeGee was taking turns, because Spunk tried to hog the fan the whole time.

Finally, Mr. Tindale looked up. His voice was really excited as he said, "Okay, here's what I got goin'. Since we want to do everything we can to help you give your gift the right way, I'm writing things up, you know, about how it works the best and all. Think you could help out by going on over to the library today and doing some research?"

"What kind of research?"

"Well, you can look up the meaning of all the words that could help us understand things better, like 'gift' and 'gifted'."

"And 'Knowing'," CeeGee added, "but that definition probably wouldn't make sense because I made it up."

"Well, you never know about a Knowing," he chuckled. "Worth a try." Mr. Tindale held up the tablet. "While you're doing that, I'll keep working on these rules for us to follow." He grazed his finger down the sheet and tapped his forehead with the eraser a few times, "Let me think...."

"Rules? What do we need rules for?" CeeGee pulled her chair back to the table, sat down and looked at him sideways.

"For you. For giving your gift."

"I hate rules. I have way too many rules in my life already. Between my mother and father, the lifeguard at the beach, Miss McGuire at the library, all the teachers at school, I am drowning in rules. I don't need any more rules."

But he insisted, "No, these will be good. I'll just get us started and then we can work 'em out together."

"How come *you* get to figure out *my* rules?" CeeGee asked, with another wary glance.

"So, I can help you give your gift, so I can help you do it the right way. Once we're done, you can keep 'em with you, so if I'm not right here you'll still know what to do."

"You said *you'd* be here for me. You said *you'd* help me."

"Celia Gene, I am trying to help you by making up these rules. Now will you please get on over to the library before I lose my patience. As we go along, we can change them around however we want. For goodness sakes, Celia Gene, you don't have to throw a hissy fit about a few good rules."

"There's no such thing as a few good rules," CeeGee muttered as she walked out the door.

CeeGee was feeling exasperated as she got on her bike and started to ride. And she sure didn't feel like going to the library again so Miss McGuire could boss her around with Library Rules the same way Mr. Tindale was trying to do with Knowing Rules. She pedaled a half a block, then put on her brakes, turned her bike around and went back to the house. She marched into the kitchen and said, "I don't want a big old list of rules. That will make me not want to give my gift at all—ever again."

Mr. Tindale jumped in his seat. "Oh my heavens, girl, you scared me out of my wits." CeeGee stood firm, her chin thrust out and her hands on her hips. "Celia Gene, for heaven's sake, there are only going to be about ten or twelve of them."

"That's way too many. And I don't want to go to the library and do research. I have things to do, things I *need* to do. Real things, not stuff I can read from some rule book or the dictionary."

"Sit down here, girl. What is going on with you?"

CeeGee sat back down and started off by telling him about meeting Ronnie Sampson on Bream Street. At first Mr. Tindale looked like he was about to scold her for going over there, but then he listened, and she could tell by his face that he knew she was in a brand-new day with her gift. He pushed his pencil and tablet aside and stayed quiet. As she continued, he got up and went to the refrigerator, pulled out a pitcher of sweet tea and glasses for the two of them, then fetched an apple and his special knife. He sat back down quietly and let her keep talking while he peeled the apple and handed slices to her. Spunk jumped up on the table, so he could be in the middle of the whole thing. They let him be, and the fan made a nice breeze, wafting back and forth over the three of them.

CeeGee went on talking. She told Mr. Tindale the whole story about Ronnie and how, at first, she was scared and wanted to leave, but then her Knowing took her back. She told him about the birds Ronnie made and how beautiful they were and that she took him the Audubon book. Then she told him about meeting Elby at the library and how he was so smart. She said Elby had a gift too, and sometimes it was hard on him like it was on her. She said she thought she had made a real friend, maybe for the first time, and she didn't feel so lonely anymore—even though she knew Mr. Tindale was her friend, too.

"I see how it is, Celie Gene. This boy is your own age—plus he has a special gift. I'm happy for you," he reached out and squeezed her shoulder. "Go on with your story now."

So, she did. She talked so long, she got tired of saying 'Mr. Tindale' over and over and started calling him Mr. T. Then he got all misty because he said Maggie May used to call him Mr. T, too. Finally, CeeGee was done.

"Celia Gene, even though you were disobedient by going over to Bream Street, this story you're tellin' me sounds like we're headin' in the right direction. And soon as you can, I want you to bring your new friend over here, what's his name, Elspeth?"

"Elby."

"Okay then, Elby, bring him on by, we'll make it a team."

"Without rules?"

"Child, you are so stubborn. We got to have something to guide us on our way. We have to know what the steps are, a way to make sure we are staying on the right path."

"You said something to guide us. A guide—that is different from rules. That is more like a map."

"Well, that's what I meant all along, for heaven's sake."

"Rules are different—rules are things that grownups keep track of so they can punish kids. Ask Danny and Davey."

"All right then, fine." Mr. T. pulled the tablet back to him, scratched out CEEGEE'S RULES at the top of the page, thought for a minute and then wrote, CEEGEE'S GUIDE FOR GIVING.

CeeGee read it over, then said the words out loud. "CeeGee's Guide for Giving." She said it again. "Okay, I can see the help in a guide." She read down the list. "There's too many here, it'll be too confusing to learn all of these, much less remember them."

Mr. T. looked his list over. "It's just a first draft, we'll work it out together. We'll work on it until it makes sense for you."

CeeGee scooted her chair around so they could both see the tablet. "So, first off," she said, "you told me the reason we are all here is to figure out our gifts and learn how to give them. So that means everyone has gifts, right? I mean I know I do, and Elby does, and you sure are a gift to me." She paused and squeezed his arm, "Now that you aren't all stuck on rules, that is. But does everyone have a gift?"

"Yep, that's what I believe. If we can recognize the truth of it and look for those gifts in others, then we can truly value them and maybe even help 'em get a little better at giving their own gifts. Like, look at all your Knowings. You are starting to see how you can be better at giving your gift. When you were a wee one, those Knowings came to you just like you told me, a fuzzy radio signal going by when you didn't know how to tune it yet. Even then, you knew to give the hug and feel the sorrow for Mrs. Jennings."

"That's right."

"So, see? Right there, your job was to try to help the living go on a little better. That's what we figured out these last weeks, but the clue was right there. My land, only six years old." He shook his head and reached over to pat CeeGee's arm.

"I never thought of it that way. So, what you are saying is if we write down what we are learning, it will help me use my gift better, and then maybe I can truly help people instead of just knowing that awful things are about to happen."

"Exactly right, child. See, getting set up with this guide will help us to understand. Since you and I have been working together, a lot of good has come out of your Knowings. Like how you helped Mike Robins get work and now he can feed his family, and Mrs. Robins has some household help, so she can rest and ease her worries for her last days. And I got myself a beautiful handmade casket."

Cee said, "I can see that about the Robins family. And even when I think about my family, I can see that my mother is giving her gifts by being a good teacher, even to the troublemaker kids, like Ronnie used to be. She saw the good in Ronnie, or at least she could see why he was so bad. And I can see how my dad is helping people find the right medicines, and how he's patient with the old folks who can't hear or understand too well. And he gave Johnny Johanssen a job, even when he didn't really want to, and now Johnny has found his gift at the soda fountain."

"So, what do you think your brothers' gifts are?" Mr. T. asked.

"My brothers are very gifted at tormenting their little sister," CeeGee answered.

"Tormenting is a good word, Celia Gene, but it does not count as a gift. Think again."

"They are very gifted at getting into trouble."

"Celia Gene."

"Okay, I'll try." CeeGee had to ponder the question for a long time before she could think of the twins as anything but ornery. Finally, she said, "Okay, Davey is a leader, kind of like my mom. When kids come over, Davey is the one that comes up with a game and assigns everyone a part. He's good at that."

"And generous?"

"I guess. He doesn't leave anyone out. He doesn't always choose the strongest or the smartest kid for the best part either. He gives everyone a chance." CeeGee paused then added, "Except me, of course."

"What about Danny?"

"Well, Danny is more like my dad. He can figure things out and he's good at math. One time, Danny figured out how to dig a tunnel down under our yard, all the way across the alley and up into the Whitcomb's yard."

"Why in blazes did he do that?"

"He and Davey and the Whitcomb boys thought if they had a tunnel they could sneak back and forth to each other's houses without anyone knowing." CeeGee shook her head and added, "Like they couldn't just sneak straight across the alley when no-body was looking, right? Anyway, Danny was the one who figured out how deep to dig, and when to turn sideways. He figured how wide it had to be and how to brace the inside so the tunnel wouldn't collapse on top of them. He figured out where to hide all the dirt they took out. It was pretty amazing, really."

"I'll say. Did they get the job done?"

"Nope. They were moving right along until, one day, Dad got into a big lather about the palm fronds that had been lying behind the shed in the backyard for weeks and told the twins to go clean them up."

"What's wrong with that?"

"Well, that was how they hid the entrance to the tunnel, with a bunch of palm fronds nailed to some two by fours."

"Oh, my land, what happened then?"

"By the time my dad started sniffing around, they'd dug all the way down and made the turn from both yards, planning to meet in the middle. But then Dad went and looked at those palm fronds himself, pulled them aside and saw the big hole in our yard and—well, you'd just better take cover.

"You know how my dad sounds like he is talking in capital let-ters sometimes? He pointed down at that hole and said, 'DANIEL AND DAVID WILLIAMSON. YOU BOYS HIGH TAIL IT

OVER HERE RIGHT NOW AND TELL ME WHAT THE
HELL IS GOING ON HERE!"'Scuse my language."

"It's all right, it was a direct quote. Go on."

"Well, once Dad got the whole story out of them, he was mad
as a hornet. He went and told Jack and Sam Whitcomb's parents,
so those boys got in trouble, too. Dad said, 'Did you boys ever think
to calculate what might happen if something very heavy, LIKE A
GARBAGE TRUCK, drove over your blasted tunnel?' They, of
course, hadn't thought of that. My dad called up Sheriff Cummings
and had him come over to the house. He looked all around the
holes and the tunnels in both yards and talked to the parents and
all the boys. Then he sent over someone from the city crew to tell
the boys how to fill the holes back in and keep checking on them
to make sure they did it right. It took them about three weeks after
school and every weekend. Plus, after that, for what seemed like
months, they couldn't go to see any of their friends or have anyone
come over. That was pure torture for all of us. But, you know, even
though my dad acted really mad, I think he was sort of impressed
that the twins tried to do it. How many boys their age would try to
do something like that, or even be able to figure out how?"

"Not many, I'd wager." Mr. T. nodded.

The whole conversation caused CeeGee to feel just a tiny bit
proud of her brothers and for a moment, she felt tempted to tell
them so. But she figured she'd get over it by the time she got home.

Once CeeGee was done with her storytelling and catching
Mr. Tindale up on all her news, they kept on talking about the
guide. What did she need to do, every time, step by step, to give her
gift the best way she could? By late afternoon they had agreed on
five steps, but CeeGee wanted to add one more, the sixth and last.

"Never Tell the Parents Anything." CeeGee stated.

"I think it's time to tell your parents what's going on with
you, child. They would understand and be a help," Mr T. urged.

"I am never, ever going to tell them a single thing about my gift, ever again. I already know what would happen. It would be just the same as before. They would think I'm a freak, and then they'd get in a big fight, and be mad at each other for weeks on end, or maybe forever. My parents want a nice, normal kid, and that's what I aim to be, far as they're concerned."

"Celia Gene, first off, who says you are not normal? As we've written right here," he stabbed at the paper with his index finger, "everyone has gifts, not just you. Besides that, you are not the same person as you were in third grade, and neither are they. Least you can do is give 'em a chance."

"Nope, not for discussion. Besides, they are my parents, not yours. I want you to let me be in charge of my own parents."

"I don't agree…"

"You don't have to, because they are *my* parents."

"Oh, all right," he said grudgingly. "I am going to try to trust you on this, Celia Gene. I am going to trust that you are growing up and you will search your head and your heart and make the right decision. But I am telling you, clear as I can, your mother and father are not who you think they are. Not anymore. And you will need them as this gift grows inside you. I won't bring it up again, but I'm saying it strong right now."

CeeGee tucked her hair behind her ear and pushed her glasses up on her nose. "Fine, now can we finish?"

"Yes, we can finish, and you can write whatever extra you want on your own guide, I will have only five on mine—and there will be nothing about parents. I got to draw the line."

Finally, they were done. CeeGee rewrote the guide on her own piece of paper so she could always have it with her, even when Mr. Tindale wasn't around.

CeeGee's Guide for Giving

1. Our job here on earth is to discover our gifts and learn how to give them. Everyone has gifts to share.

2. We must give our gifts in a kind and generous way, and never try to make ourselves feel big by making others feel small.

3. We can't judge anyone because we don't know everything. In the whole of things, we are no more than a tiny crab, in a tiny tide pool, on the shore of an ocean, with all the heavens beyond.

4. We must always look for silver linings because things that seem bad at first can turn out good in the end.

5. If we decide to change the direction we are headed, we can change our entire future.

   AND Never tell the parents anything.

Chapter Eleven

The next morning at breakfast, the three Williamson children waited impatiently for Bobbie to scramble some eggs. Danny and Davey could not stop squirming in their seats.

"Come on, Mom, we need to go!"

"We start on the float today."

Bobbie turned from the stove to stare them down. "Fine," she said. "Danny, you want to finish up the cooking here or just go on without any breakfast?"

"Oh, Mom, just hurry, okay?" Davey said.

"Watch it," Bobbie said over her shoulder as she turned back to the stove.

It was the third week in June, the time when the whole town of Southport started to get ready for the Fourth of July Parade. On the fourth, every resident, including the police, would either be at the parade or in the parade. CeeGee had always thought it would be the perfect day for a bunch of thieves to sail a boat over to Magdalena Island, rob all the homes they wanted, carry their plunder right back on board and sail away. No one would be around to stop them. People on the island never thought to lock their houses, and that included tourists, so the thieves could probably get into a few rental cottages and hotel rooms as well.

Once Bobbie finished making breakfast, CeeGee and her brothers ate as fast as they could. Then they jumped on their bikes and rode to the gym, with CeeGee pedaling hard to keep up. The gym was crowded, and at first, it made CeeGee uncomfortable. All the noise and movement reminded her of the years she had been so closed up at school to keep out the hum of the radio, and how it had made her so alone. She didn't feel any hum at all now and figured that since she'd been working with Mr. T. she'd be able to handle a Knowing in case one came along anyway, so she relaxed and looked around for Elby. Once she saw him walking toward her, she ran over to him and they went to sit on the bleachers.

Kids of every age in Southport had a big role in the parade because the students had their own Fourth of July float. The float had been the same for years and years, and it was CeeGee's favorite in the whole parade. Her dad's Town Club had come up with the idea years ago, when CeeGee was just a toddler. The men in the Town Club still took turns with the driving, but the high school students got to put it all together and take it apart for storage every year. The elementary school kids got to ride on it and four junior high school kids marched in front of the float carrying school and town flags. The school colors were blue and white, and the mascot was, not surprisingly, a leaping dolphin.

All the teachers and coaches had to do was put a big tarp over the gym floor, get the sections of the float out of storage, and watch over the kids while they put the pieces together. The gym had big double doors on each side, so when the assembly was done they could roll the float right out of the gym, hook the sections together and put it in line at the top of Beacon Street. CeeGee wasn't one of the junior high flag carriers, so she just hoped to tag along with her brothers and Elby and help out at the gym.

The teachers had already covered the floor, laid out the sections of the float in order and set the tools next to each section so the students could get to work. At the front of the float was a motorized cart, the kind that tourists rented to ride around town.

Panels of plywood, painted red and shaped like a tug boat, were added to the sides of the cart with the name "Lil' TOOT" written in black on each side. There were openings for windows, and the float driver would sit in there tooting a special horn and shooting steam out of a little chimney on the top. Behind Lil' TOOT, a string of small boat trailers were all being hooked together with a red rowboat perched on top of each one. To hide the trailers, the students attached long, wavy strips of wood to each side, painted blue and white to look like the boats were riding little waves in a choppy surf.

On parade day, the little kids, as many as could fit, sat in those five boats and waved like movie stars as Lil' TOOT wove along down Beacon Street. All the parents and tourists shouted and clapped and waved back at them. The float reminded CeeGee of a mother duck with all her ducklings stringing along behind her, which her dad told her was exactly the idea the men in the Town Club had when they came up with the idea.

CeeGee and Elby sat in the bleachers together watching the construction. They didn't need any more workers, as there were probably twenty or so on the gym floor. After about an hour, Elby had to go. Parent duty, he told CeeGee and grimaced as he trotted off. CeeGee kept watching all the meaningless parts and pieces on the floor of the gym get lifted up, hooked together, trimmed on the sides and gradually turn into Lil' TOOT.

There was a weight room off to the side of the gym and kids were coming in and out of the door after doing their summer training with the coaches. They all stopped to check out the construction for a while then left. CeeGee watched the comings and goings, feeling like she belonged with these kids more than she ever had. She wasn't scared of being around them anymore. She was getting used to being in her own skin. Then, just as if she'd hit the start button, she went and had a Knowing right there in the bleachers. The light came really quick, busting through clear as day, and went right into her. Then—bam—it was over.

The Knowing was about Billy Joe Jones, a person she would never try to help out in any way at all if she had a choice in the matter. And Kim Soon, someone she would gladly help in a second for any reason whatsoever. CeeGee had known Billy Joe since he was the runt in her kindergarten class and everyone teased and picked on him. As he got older, he got bigger and bigger until he was big enough to tease people back, which is exactly what he did. These days, Billy Joe was always lifting weights and showing off his muscles, and saying things like, "I am the man!" He went straight from being a runt to a bully, sure enough.

Kim Soon was the newest student at her school. His family had moved to Magdalena Island from South Korea and opened Southport's first and only Asian restaurant, the Asian Pearl. It was a nice little place, small and clean, and Kim worked there at night and on weekends along with the rest of his family. CeeGee thought Kim was special, coming to a strange country, learning English and all of his lessons so fast and starting a new business. Plus, he was very polite to everyone. But he was shy; he kept his head down when he walked, and he didn't speak unless he had to.

CeeGee looked around and saw Billy Joe coming out of the weight training room. She got up to meet him but wasn't at all sure what she'd say when she did.

"Take that, and that!" Billy Joe said, dancing around and punching at the air. "Pow, Pow, Pow!"

"Hey, watch out, Billy Joe!" CeeGee ducked.

"Hey there, Williamson. Watch this. Boom, Bam, Pow, Pow!"

"Yeah, yeah, I know. You're the man. Can you please let up for a second?"

"Can't ya' see I'm workin' out here, girl?" He stopped and looked across the gym where he saw Kim Soon walking along the far wall, heading for the doors to the outside. Billy Joe's face went dark as his eyes followed Kim, who had his head tucked down into his chest, his coal black hair falling over his forehead and his thin arms thrust into his pockets.

"You know, I'm gonna have to teach that Soon kid a thing or two, let him know who's in charge here in the U.S. of A." He shot a few jabs in Kim's direction, then slapped himself in the chest. "Billy Joe Jones, that's who!" He watched as Kim disappeared out the door and then turned back to CeeGee. "Stinkin' teacher's pet, I'll show him. Gotta' keep these foreigners in their place. Know what I mean?"

CeeGee looked over the top of her glasses at Billy Joe, then pushed them back up on her nose. She was just about to tell him that he was a bully and an idiot, and he was going to get exactly what he deserved, when she remembered the second rule of her guide—we must give our gifts in a kind and generous way. "You know what, Billy Joe," she said, trying her best to sound kind and generous, "I've gotten to know Kim a little bit, and I like him. I think he's really nice. Why would you want to hurt him?"

Billy Joe looked at her in amazement. "What? Williamson, he's not one of us."

CeeGee went on. "It's just…Billy Joe, my family came from somewhere else, and I bet yours did, too. How would you like it if someone picked on you just because of where you came from, where you were born, or your family?" He seemed to be listening, so she added, "I mean, I know you're the man and all now, but I remember when you were little, and how you got picked on and teased." Billy Joe looked like he had a flash of memory, and maybe just a blink of sympathy. CeeGee hurried on, "So…why would you want to put someone else through that, you know? Besides that, little people aren't always weak or slow. Remember David and Goliath? Remember the Tortoise and the Hare? Maybe Kim is stronger than he looks."

Billy Joe threw back his shoulders and stared at her. "What? That slanty-eyed little mouse? Come on, Williamson, look at him; he's as skinny as you are, and his hair looks like a dirty broom." He raised his fists to his chin and ducked left and right, getting back into a fighting mood. "That's right, the kid is a mouse and I'm the big ole' alley cat come to show him who's in charge of this neighborhood." He leaned into CeeGee and added, "Heck, it's almost embarrassin', you know? Hardly even a fair fight. I wouldn't do it if it weren't for me being the man and all. But we gotta' keep control. This kid can't be comin' over here thinkin' he got rights, thinkin' he's got a place."

"Billy Joe, let me just say, and this may sound kind of strange, but I've got a feeling that Kim *is* different like you say, but maybe not in the way you're thinking. Maybe you could act different, too. See what happens then. Maybe it could turn out better."

Billy Joe gave CeeGee a gentle punch in the shoulder. "Hey, kid, don't you worry. I got it all under control." He danced in a circle with his fists over his head.

CeeGee ran through what she had said in her mind. She'd done her best to make sure she got all the way to number five. She tried to help Billy Joe see the direction he was headed, so if he wanted to, he could change direction and change his future. Fact was, he didn't want to. "Right, Billy Joe, it's up to you." CeeGee moved around him to let him pass, and he danced across the gym, pulled open the heavy door and stepped outside. CeeGee couldn't help but smile just a little as the door slammed shut behind him.

When CeeGee got home, her mother was waiting at the kitchen table. She had put two Dr. Peppers out, with a dish of lime wedges, a bowl of salsa and some tortilla chips. CeeGee knew from the food that her mother had something important to say. She sat down warily and asked, "What's up, Momma?"

Bobbie reached out and touched her cheek. "I've been waiting for you because I wanted to be here to tell you myself, darlin'. Here, have some chips." She pushed the bowl over and waited while CeeGee ate a few, then said, "I know you've been a good friend to the Robins family, Celia Gene, and I know how you helped them find Rosa and Juan to lend a hand while Mrs. Robins has been so sick. Rosa came over here herself this morning and told me all about what a help you've been." Bobbie paused.

CeeGee got scared her mother would go further into her secret life but decided to stay quiet and let her keep going.

"Rosa also told me that Mrs. Robins passed last night."

"Oh no, Momma."

"Rosa came here because she wanted you to know. She told me how it all happened, so I could share it with you, because she knows how much you care about this family."

CeeGee brushed away the tears that were starting to come. "How did it happen?"

Bobbie reached out and touched her cheek again. "You go right ahead and cry, darlin', but really, it was all right. You know Mrs. Robins was so ill, and it had been lingering for so, so long. Rosa said she was hanging on for her family, afraid that they would all be in trouble without her. You know with four kids and Mike being out of work for a while, she was worried for their futures. But Rosa said over the last few weeks Mrs. Robins could tell that Mike had really set things right with all of his casket work coming in and how he had built his home workshop. She knew he was going to make enough money to keep the family going, and he'd be nearby for the kids while he worked. Rosa told me that it was thanks to you and Mr. Tindale that she and Juan had been hired to help with the house and the kids and the garden. So, Mrs. Robins could see that everything was in order."

CeeGee was nodding solemnly as her mother spoke. She could see Mrs. Robins, thin as a ghost, walking through the house and garden those last days, checking on each child before she lay down in exhaustion on the lawn chair or sofa. What must it have meant to her to know that the kids had Rosa every day to help with baths and dinner? That Rosa was there to love them and hold them. And that Juan would take care of the yard and the garden, so Mike could keep on with his work.

Bobbie went on, "So, last night she had a fine dinner with her family. Rosa said that after dinner, she put on her favorite night-dress, kissed everyone and told them how much she loved them. Then she went to bed and passed peacefully in her sleep. If a body has to go, she went calm, filled with love and loving. We can't ask for much more."

CeeGee realized how that was true. To know things are in order, and to be able to say a loving goodbye and then to pass on peacefully—that would be a good leaving. "Momma, thanks for being here to tell me all this."

"I am here for you always, darlin', for whatever you may need. I hope you know that."

"I do, Momma. I think I want to go to my room now."

☆☆☆☆

For the next week, CeeGee, Mr. Tindale, Mike, and Juan and Rosa Leon spent all their time getting ready for Mrs. Robins' funeral. The Leons thought of everything that needed to be done and stayed real calm and steady. On Saturday morning, they worked together to set up the carport for the ceremony. Mike put a door over two sawhorses to lay out all the food that people had brought and were still bringing. Mr. T. brought one of Maggie May's beautiful cloths to put over the door so it looked like a nice table. Bobbie helped CeeGee make two dozen of the special Williamson Family Deviled Eggs. The Leons arranged the food, made punch, watched out for the kids and even met people at the end of the drive to welcome them, many bringing bouquets of flowers to add to the space. Rosa spent the whole day with one or another of the Robins' four kids on her hip, and they hung on to her for comfort.

Mike wasn't a churchgoing man, but he asked the pastor from the Leon's church to come help him say the right words about his wife's passing. The pastor had talked to Mike, Juan and Rosa, and made some notes, so he did a fine job.

The Sandwith Brothers returned the model casket Mike had just completed for their show room, so he could lay his wife to rest in it. Mike promised he'd build them a new one right away. Meanwhile, they would display Mr. Tindale's oak casket. Carl and Bobbie came to the funeral and told CeeGee they were sad about Mrs. Robins, but proud of her for being such a big help.

After the funeral, when everyone had left, Mr. Tindale and CeeGee stayed on to help clean up the carport and put Mike's shop back in order. After a while, Mike said to them, "You know, it's a good thing I set up this here home workshop. Now, even though I got work to do, I can be near the kids, which gives my mind some peace since I'm their only parent. And all the work I got with the funeral home, it's put the ship right again. And the two of you, the way you introduced me to Rosa and Juan to help out around here, it's made all the difference. It's been a hard time, with the Mrs. sick for so long and all, but without all you two done for me, I'd never have been able to get through it. It would have been too much. I think I would have come apart." He bowed his head as the tears came.

As he said all this, CeeGee laid her hand over the place on her chest that had hurt as far back as she could remember. She had always felt that her Knowings, especially the awful ones about death, had left a hole in her heart, causing her sorrow, regret and grief. It had been too much for a child, and like Mr. Tindale said, she'd been too young to know how to help anyone. But, as

Mike Robins spoke, she felt her heart stitch over and heal. There had been another death in Southport, and CeeGee had known it was coming, but this time she'd been able to use her gift to help everyone get through the hard time a little easier. She threw her arms around Mike's neck and said, "Oh, Mr. Robins, thank you so much."

Before Mike Robins could ask why she was thanking him, Mr. Tindale stepped up to Mike and put an arm around his shoulder. "What Celia Gene's trying to say is you've helped her understand that good things can come right along with things that seem so bad. We never know along the way how the pieces will all fit together, or when. But sometimes those unexpected good things make a sort of silver lining, to wrap up the whole of it nice and sweet like." Then he nodded at CeeGee and gave her a little wink. "We're glad, Mike, that we could be here for the time you needed us."

As for Mr. T., he had everything ready for his passing too, and CeeGee had relaxed about it like he told her to. She knew he'd been to the doctor to get everything checked out and he was taking his medicines like he was supposed to. He was eating right and had Rosa to help him with the house, so he wasn't so tired. His leg was bothering him, so he couldn't get out and walk as much as he'd like, but other than that, it seemed like his life was pretty darn good. Most of all, he acted like he was glad to be alive instead of always being miserable about missing Maggie May. He told CeeGee that now he could understand how her gift had worked just right with him. She told him where he was headed, and he listened to what she said and decided to change direction. Now he wasn't headed that way anymore. He was living out what was left of his life fully, happily and with purpose. "Free will," he said, "simple as that."

Chapter Twelve

A week later, at Sunday dinner, the twins couldn't wait to report on all the excitement they'd seen at the baseball field that day.

As they passed around the vegetable platter Danny said, "Mom and Dad, there was a fight!"

"But we weren't in on it," Davey added quickly.

"We saw it though," Danny said.

"What fight? Where?" Carl asked.

"It was at the baseball field," Danny answered.

"Right next to the bleachers, behind the junior high school," Davey interrupted.

Danny elbowed him and went on, "Everyone was there for the game, and right after it was over we saw this crowd of kids, so we went over to see."

"Yeah, but we weren't in on it or anything." Davey added again.

"Yes, Davey, we got that the first time," Bobbie said.

"Anyway," Danny went on, "it was Billy Joe Jones and that new kid, Kim Soon."

CeeGee stopped with her fork halfway to her mouth and held her breath.

"Yeah, from the restaurant."

"The family from Korea, right? The Asian Pearl," Carl said. "Go on."

Davey picked up the story where Danny had left off. "We asked the kids who were already there what was going on, and they said that Billy Joe had been picking on Kim for a while, telling him he ought to go back where he came from."

"Oh, how disgraceful." Bobbie said. "That family is such a gift to Southport—good hardworking people and business owners."

"Yeah, and we never had decent Asian food before they came here," said Carl.

Bobbie shook her head, "Imagine saying such things to that dear boy, he must have been devastated."

"Mom. Kim was all over Billy Joe," Davey said.

"Really?"

"He was. Kim had him ducking for cover. You should've seen it. Kim had all these amazing fight moves, like jumping up in the air and kicking with his feet and..."

"Yeah, and he made this noise," Danny interrupted, "like *EEEahhh*, every time he laid in to Billy Joe." Danny held one hand in front of his face, then switched it back and forth like lightning. "Whish, whish, whish!"

Davey said, "Mom, in like three minutes Kim had Billy Joe on the ground begging for mercy."

"Will wonders never cease," Carl said. "So, that bully got exactly what he deserved."

"Tell us, did Kim grant Billy Joe mercy?" Bobbie asked.

"Yeah, and Kim was so cool about it. He acted like a prince or something. Look." Danny got up from the table and stood with his legs wide apart and his hands on his hips. "Master Jones, from now on, I ask that you lespect my lights in this fine country as I lespect yours. Get it, *respect* my *rights?*"

"Yes," Bobbie nodded, "Kim has a Korean accent, we get that."

"Now, sit down, please." Carl told him.

Davey went on. "At the end of the fight, everyone was cheering and clapping for Kim."

"Yeah, and Billy Joe looked like a whipped dog."

CeeGee exhaled a great sigh of relief. Her Knowing was complete, and thanks to her brothers, she got to hear the end of the story, right in front of her family, without anyone getting worried half to death or finding out her secret. Who would imagine Danny and Davey could do something so special for her? She couldn't wait to tell Mr. T. She'd already talked through the Knowing with him, and he said that except for being glad in advance that Billy Joe was going to get whipped, she did pretty good. He'd told her, "Even though someone may seem to deserve a punishment, it's not our part to be glad about it. That's exactly how wrong-headed Billy Joe was about Kim. You are kinder than that, Celia Gene."

Fourth of July had finally arrived, and people were lined up on the sidewalks of Beacon Street six deep to see the parade. Some of the stores had balconies above their entry doors, so the owners and their friends and family got to stand up there and see better than anyone. The mayor was on the movie theater balcony, because he was the judge for the best floats. CeeGee and the twins had spent years trying to get their Dad to put a balcony over the front door of the Triple S, but he said it was ridiculous. "Why would I spend all that money so the three of you can stand up there and show off one day a year? Ridiculous."

This year, though, the talk of the town was the fight, not the floats. People lined up to pat Kim on the back, and Billy Joe wandered up and down the sidewalk on Beacon Street looking completely lost, like he'd landed on a strange new planet without a map. No one was paying any attention to him except to whisper and point as he went by.

After the parade, CeeGee was riding her bicycle to the library, when she passed by the ball park. She could see Billy Joe sitting in the bleachers, his head hung low. This was where the fight happened, CeeGee remembered, a place where he started out a bully and ended up a clown. She turned onto the path to the field, left her bike and walked toward the bleachers where Billy Joe sat with his back to her. He had his arms on his knees and his head dropped down.

CeeGee wasn't sure what to do. Should she try to talk to Billy Joe, somehow let him know one person was sorry for him? She started to walk towards him, but just then, she saw Kim Soon walking across the other side of the baseball field toward Billy Joe. She stepped back and crouched behind a water fountain along the path. With his head down, Billy Joe didn't see Kim coming, but when Kim started to climb up the bleachers, Billy Joe looked up and got stiff. Kim stopped a few rows down from him and started to talk, and pretty soon Billy Joe relaxed and just listened to what Kim had to say. After a minute or two, Kim stepped up next to Billy Joe, then reached out and put his hand on Billy Joe's shoulder. Billy Joe ducked his head, then Kim sat down next to him and they went on talking. CeeGee quietly moved under them so she could hear what they were saying.

"…say that again. What's it called?"

"Tae Kwon Do." Kim spelled it out for Billy Joe. "I began to study at four years old and had lessons three times every week. I earned my black belt at the age of ten."

"Wow, we don't work that hard around here. A black belt, what's that?"

"That is the highest level, so I am very good at Tae Kwon Do, you see? Very highly trained."

"Yeah, I get that now. No wonder you whipped me so bad. Hey, you think you could teach me?"

"I could, but Tae Kwon Do is not used to start a fight, Master Jones, it is only for defense."

"Yeah, well, the way things are going I may be needing that," said Billy Joe, sounding dejected.

"So, if I teach you Tae Kwon Do, you teach me proper English?"

"Right, like you need my help." Billy Joe shook his head. "But sure, I'll try. Listen, did you want to come here? Or did the parents drag you?"

"Dragging? No, we all came on ship."

"Sorry, just an American expression. Guess I could teach you some of those, too." Billy Joe punched him in the shoulder and Kim gently punched him back. "Startin' with, you can just call me Billy Joe, I sure ain't no Master. A ship—how was that? I've never been out of Texas…"

CeeGee quietly left, her heart swelling with feelings she could not even name. Her Knowing didn't tell her Kim would be so generous and forgiving, that was just the kind of boy he was. But how many his age would be so kind after what had happened? She felt like she had just seen the beginning of a real silver lining for Billy Joe. And she wondered if seeing it for herself had been part of the Knowing, part of how things were going to be different now.

CeeGee got back on her bike and rode over to the library, and when she went inside she noticed Miss McGuire over at the book checkout counter. She was drawing something on a big sheet of paper, then mumbling and erasing and angrily brushing off the eraser bits. CeeGee walked over to see what she was doing. "How's it going, Miss McGuire?"

"You know, Celia Gene, I am most awfully tired of hearing that, *Miss* McGuire, Miss, Miss, Miss, Miss, Miss, Miss, Miss."

"You want me to call you something else?"

"No. Oh, I don't know. Celia Gene, I am just in a knot. Our community has outgrown this public library. We need a space for you older children to study quietly and another space for the little children to have story time. But all we have is this one big space and no money to make it any different. I can't figure out how to fix it. I keep drawing and drawing my ideas, but I have no way to make any of my ideas happen."

CeeGee looked at the upside-down sketches for a while and then went ahead and brought up the other thing that seemed to be on Miss McGuire's mind. "So, how are things going with your Knight in Shining Armor?"

"Oh, I don't even want to talk about it, Celia Gene. I just don't know what more I can do to make my knight appear. I have done all I can with my hair and my clothes and going to church and all... I am just sick and tired of the whole subject. I may as well give up and be a shriveled up old maid."

CeeGee felt the light coming, right there in the middle of the conversation. She was getting used to having her Knowings by now, so she just let this one fill her up. She knew no one else could see, plus now she had her guide to help her know what to do. Miss McGuire chattered on while CeeGee absorbed the light.

"...Truth is, I don't believe there is a single knight anywhere in Southport. Maybe in the entire Texas Coastal Bend."

CeeGee, having just learned what Miss McGuire's future actually could be, dared to comment. "Now that you mention it, I always thought the idea of a white horse galloping down Beacon Street and some guy in a metal suit of armor sweeping you up and riding away with you was sort of scary."

"Oh, you're right, I suppose. I never thought about the scary part." Miss McGuire brushed more bits of eraser from her drawing.

"Miss McGuire, I always wondered—if you are waiting for a knight, does that make you a princess?"

"Obviously not." Miss McGuire stood up straight and held out her thin arms. "Look at me, is this any kind of princess?" Her shoulders sagged, and she looked at CeeGee helplessly. "Fact is, it's all just my silly dream."

CeeGee let it be quiet for a while and Miss McGuire went back to her sketches. CeeGee knew she had a job to do, and it wasn't an easy one. How could she help the stubborn, know it all, bossy librarian see what her real future might be instead of the made-up one she'd believed in for so long? CeeGee finally said, "Even if there aren't any knights in Southport, Miss McGuire, there are a lot of nice people here. Your age even."

"Ancient, you mean? A comment like that does not make the situation one bit better, Celia Gene, not one little bit, thank you very much."

"Sorry." CeeGee waited a minute and tried again. "Miss McGuire, I wonder, if you were looking for a real man, instead of that fairy tale knight, what kind of a man would you like him to be?"

"I have no earthly idea." Miss McGuire looked lost and dejected.

CeeGee prodded, "Well, you're an extra good reader and all, so he'd have to be a reader too, right?"

"Yes, I suppose so. Oh, all right, let me see." She tapped her pencil on the counter. "What else? I think I'd like him to be a bit of a dreamer, you know? And perhaps a little shy, so he'd need somebody to encourage him. Like me."

"That sounds good, Miss McGuire. That sounds just right for you."

"And travel," she went on, getting into the swing of it, "I'd like a man who wanted to look at travel books and plan trips together. I've always wanted to do that. It would be great fun to go explore the world with someone who is curious the way I am." Miss McGuire put her elbows on the checkout counter and stared off into space with the faraway look she always got when she talked about her knight. Only now she was imagining a real live man.

"Miss McGuire, that sounds like a very nice man. I bet you anything you could meet somebody like that. Just think, he probably wouldn't even care about your hair or your clothes, or even if you go to church."

"My heavens, no church?" She leaned toward CeeGee and whispered, "Well, that's a bit of a relief. To tell you the truth, I'm a bit tired of the whole church business myself. I mean, how many times does a woman of my intelligence need to read the Good Book before I get the point, you know?"

"But, I bet you have some real interesting opinions about what you read from the Bible and other books, and I bet that's what he'd like to know. What it all means to you. I think you'd have an awful lot to share."

Miss McGuire started to fan her face as if she were suddenly hot. "Oh, Celia Gene, do you really think so? That's so very kind of you to say that. I do have so many opinions, so many ideas. It would be nice if I could meet someone who was interested in learning these things about me."

"You know, Miss McGuire, sometimes if you just change the direction you're headed, you can change your whole future."

"Why, Celia Gene, that's a very big idea for such a young girl. I'll have to think on that. Yes, I will."

"Well, I better get to reading from your list," CeeGee said.

"Yes, dear, you get right to work. I will think about all you said, I surely will. But at this moment, once again, I must try to solve the problem with this library. It will be a simple miracle if I ever get it done in the proper way."

While CeeGee sat at the table trying unsuccessfully to concentrate on her reading, she found herself thinking about Ronnie Sampson, and how good he was at his carvings and all the things his future might hold if he could just get out and live in a bigger world than his shady carport. His world wasn't make believe, but it was just as small and hopeless as Miss McGuire's. Then she had an idea. She'd take Ronnie a few more art books from the library. If he had some books to look at, he might see that there were artists all over the world and he could be one of them. Maybe he would start to think about learning art even before she could figure out a plan to help him finish high school.

She went over to the art section and looked at every book. She found one she liked on drawing techniques, then another on art history with the pictures of all the famous paintings through the ages. She picked out a third one that had stories about the lives of famous artists and how they learned to do their work. She decided not to pick out anything about making movies or cartoons, because that part was too far in the future and it wouldn't make sense to anyone but her and Elby—and Mr. T.

When she went up to the desk to check the books out, Miss McGuire seemed to be in a little bit better spirits and started to pepper CeeGee with questions. "Why, Celia Gene, I didn't know you had an interest in art? When did this happen? Is it distracting you from reading my list? Where are you on the list, my child?"

"No, ma'am, I'm doing fine on the list. I am up to the *L's*, Harper Lee. I am reading *To Kill a Mockingbird*."

"That is a perfectly suitable book for your age group. Seems like young Scout was just about your age, if I remember right. Awful title though, in my informed opinion. What kind of message does that send to children? You must make sure those brothers of yours don't get their grubby hands on Miss Lee's book, or in short order there will be no mockingbirds left on the whole of Magdalena Island."

"Yes, ma'am, I'll watch out for that," CeeGee said with a smile.

Miss McGuire took the books and CeeGee's library card and got ready to check them out. "Now back to the subject at hand. What has prompted your sudden interest in art?"

"The books aren't for me. I'm taking them over to Ronnie Sampson's house. He likes art, but he's stuck in a wheelchair with nothing to do."

"Why, isn't that nice of you. And, of course you know, young lady, if you are the one to check them out it is your responsibility to have them back here by the due date."

"Yes, ma'am."

"Well then, now that we have that clearly understood, I must add that taking these books is a very kind gesture, Celia Gene."

The moment Miss McGuire said those two words, 'kind gesture,' it reminded CeeGee of her Knowing about the librarian, and even though she hadn't talked things out with Elby or Mr. T. yet, the words gave her an idea. "I bet there are lots of people on the island like Ronnie, Miss McGuire. People who would like some books to read but can't get in here so easy to pick them up. Why, let's see, there are all the people in the senior home—and at the medical center. And then Ronnie, of course. And Mr. Tindale's leg is acting up and he can't get around so good anymore. I bet he'd like some books. Oh, and what about Ernest Hughes?"

"Ernest Hughes. Isn't he that strange man who lives down by the saltwater pond?"

"Yes, ma'am, but he's not so strange really; he just doesn't like to be around a lot of people. Did you know he comes to town to get his groceries at night, right before the Shop and Save closes, so he doesn't have to see anybody?"

"I did not know that, but Ernest Hughes is no concern of mine."

"Yes, but he's real interesting. Did you know he invented the surf chair?"

"What in heaven's name is the surf chair?" Miss McGuire sat down behind the counter.

"It's for surf fishing, and Ernest Hughes always uses it when he goes. It's this big, tall chair—sort of like a lifeguard chair, only with wheels on the back and handles on the top. He built it so that he could tilt it back and push it in front of him all the way out to a sandbar. Once he gets out there, he tilts it back up and climbs up a ladder to a nice padded seat. At the top, he has two covered boxes filled with ice, one for bait and one for his catch, so he can sit and fish, nice and comfortable, until his bait runs out."

"My land, I have to admit, that is quite clever. I never did understand why all these islanders struggle out to those sandbars and haul their fish in to shore one at a time. This chair seems highly efficient if you ask me."

"My dad wouldn't agree with you there, Miss McGuire. My dad says the surf chair is a travesty—which made no sense to me until I looked it up in the dictionary."

"Good, dear. And what did you learn?"

"Well, at first looking it up didn't help much because the definitions of *travesty* were all words I didn't know either, like *caricature* and *parody* and *sham* and *farce*. So, I had to go and look up all of those worlds up until I finally understood what *travesty* meant."

"What did you discover that it means, Celia Gene?"

"It means just what my dad thinks—that using the surf chair is plain wrong and it breaks the rules of the sport. He thinks the whole point of surf fishing is that while you are hauling your catch into shore, each fish has a fighting chance to get off the line and escape back to sea."

"Your father is a man of many opinions, but there is no denying this surf chair is a clever idea. No denying that."

"I always hoped Mr. Hughes would let me sit up in the chair and cast a few times, but he never did. He'd have to talk to me to do that, and like I said, he doesn't talk much."

"But you think he would like some books to read?"

"I do. I think really hard ones—the kind you like. And I think Ronnie Sampson is ready to learn about art as fast as he can. And, of course, Mr. Tindale already knows a lot, but he always wants to know more." CeeGee waited for Miss McGuire to consider how many interesting people there were on the island who needed good books to read. "You know what else I heard?"

"What, my dear?"

CeeGee leaned on the counter and lowered her voice. "I heard that Ernest Hughes might be a relative of Howard Hughes. You know Howard Hughes, that really rich and famous man?"

"Celia Gene, I know perfectly well who Howard Hughes is."

"So, if Howard Hughes is a relative, maybe Ernest is rich, too. Only he doesn't want us to know and that's why he keeps off to himself."

"And how is that any of my concern, child?"

CeeGee could not believe her own genius as she connected the dots between her Knowing and this exact moment. Elby and his deductive reasoning must be rubbing off on her. "Because if you're looking for more money for the library, then maybe some of these people would help if the library meant something important to them. *If* you took them some books and stayed to visit for a while, *then* you could tell them all about your remodel plans and who knows where that might lead?"

Miss McGuire's face perked up. "Why, that is a lovely idea. I could share some books and all my wonderful plans for the library with people who wouldn't know about it otherwise. And I am quite the cook, you know. Maybe I could take along some homemade brownies. Yes, I could designate certain days of the week to go visit, in the evenings, and they could look forward to it—the good books and the brownies. And me, of course."

"Miss McGuire, that is such a good idea. That's what you can call it—Books and Brownies! I can't believe you thought of that. You know, if this is what you have planned, maybe you would like to take these art books to Ronnie Sampson instead of me, just to get started? Ronnie's kind of a grump, but he carves really, really good models of birds. Maybe he would show them to you, if you mentioned that I told you about his bird carvings. And if you are real nice to him."

"Yes, of course, dear, bird carvings."

CeeGee quit talking because she could see Miss McGuire was already off somewhere in her mind, planning for her new adventure.

Chapter Thirteen

CeeGee left the library and checked her watch. She was meeting Elby at the Triple S for a root beer float, but she was early, so first she rode over to Ronnie's house on Bream Street and told him she had just been to the library and talked to Miss McGuire. She said Miss McGuire would be coming over with some books soon, and maybe some brownies, too.

"Who is she, a cop?" Ronnie asked, setting a nearly finished bird down in his lap.

"No, she's our Southport public librarian. I told her about you and how good you are at carving birds and stuff. She is going to start taking books to people who can't come to the library so easy, so I told her you might like some art books."

"I found that Audubon book you brought me on the table over there," he pointed in the direction of his dart board. "That guy is completely amazing. I don't know how he did that. And who knew there were that many different birds on this here earth?"

"Have you carved any new birds since you looked at the book?"

"No, I'm still finishing up this last one," he held it up to her. "After I get this done, I'm thinking I want to try and draw some birds, maybe even paint some, like he did."

"Wow, I can't wait to see that."

"Well, you'll have to wait a while, cause I ain't got no paints or brushes yet. Took me years to get all these knives together. So, why didn't you just bring the new books on over here with you now?"

"Well…" CeeGee kept thinking as she was talking, "Well… Miss McGuire, she wants to fix up the library, and she wants special study places for kids and teenagers, and she likes art, too. So, I told her about your birds, and I thought maybe… I thought maybe she could tell you all about the library plans, and you could show her your birds and then she'd decide she'd like to put them in her new library."

"Doubt it. You know, I'm not much for chit chat," Ronnie reminded her. "And since you are the only person who's ever seen these birds—even though you think they're good, you ain't exactly an art expert, are you? I'm not so sure how good they are."

"Well, no, I am not an expert—and neither is Miss McGuire, and neither are you. I'm not making any predictions here, after all. We'll just see how it goes, okay?" She paused a moment, then added, "I also want you to know Miss McGuire is pretty bossy, but this thing she's trying to do with the books and the brownies, she's trying to be nice. So, Ronnie, you'll be nice back to her, right?"

"Whatever," Ronnie said and went back to his bird.

CeeGee rode over to the Triple S to meet Elby, but he wasn't there yet. She looked around for an empty booth and saw Alice Adams and Buster McCall. Alice and Buster were seniors at Southport High. Alice was a cheerleader and Buster was a football star. The two of them had been going steady since forever and always had their hands all over each other. They were constantly kissing, whispering in each other's ears and wrapping their arms around each other like two rag dolls. CeeGee thought it was disgusting. Her dad had told them to straighten up more times than she could count, but they acted this way everywhere, and nothing anyone said or did could stop them. She got a booth as far away from Alice and Buster as she could.

CeeGee saw Elby come in and waved him over. His family had been on vacation, so she hadn't seen him since before the Fourth of July. They had a lot to catch up on—the whole story about Billy Joe and Kim Soon, Mrs. Robins passing away, Miss McGuire's change of heart and getting more art books to Ronnie. Plus, her new Guide for Giving and how Mr. T. wanted Elby to come over and meet him. Catching up on all this news kept them so busy that at first neither one of them even noticed Alice and Buster smooching away in another booth, which was a relief.

Once they were all caught up, Elby said, "Who are those people over there?"

CeeGee turned around to see Buster's face buried in Alice's neck. "Just don't look, it's Alice and Buster; they are incorrigible."

"Good word."

"Yeah, I looked up synonyms until I found one especially for them."

"What words did you start with?"

"Stuff like *hopeless* and *incurable.*"

"Those are good. We could add *inveterate.*"

"And maybe *nauseating.*"

"Apt." Elby reached up and covered the left side of his face with his hand, so he wouldn't have to see Alice and Buster anymore and went on, "So, to continue unabated, I'd really like to meet Mr. Tindale. That was very kind of him to suggest that you bring me over. Can we go?"

"Sure."

"Now?" Elby looked hopeful.

"You don't want to get your float first?"

"Not so much."

"Okay, if you want. Why not?"

This time Elby had his own bike with him and the two of them set off. Again, CeeGee had a feeling of monumental change.

The only time she could remember riding a bike with other kids was when she tried to tag along with her brothers. She would pedal along behind them, but they would go so fast she could never keep up. Finally, she'd see them disappear on down the road and she would just give up. Here was a friend, a real friend, riding along beside her, happy to be with her.

When they arrived at Mr. Tindale's, they found him on the porch fanning himself with a newspaper. He lit up like a Fourth of July firecracker when he saw them coming down the street and waved and called out, "Why, hello there, Celia Gene! This must be your new friend Elsmore."

CeeGee stopped to pull the mail from the box and Elby climbed the steps to the front porch.

Elby went right up to Mr. T. and, like he did with her dad, put his hand out politely. "Elby. Elby Smith, sir. Very nice to meet you," he said as they shook hands.

"Why, sorry about that, and nice to meet you as well. Can you spell it for me, please?"

"E-L-B-Y, sir."

"Thank you, now I'll get it straight. Sorry I can't get up to shake your hand, but my bad leg is acting up lately, so I'd best stay put."

"That's fine, sir, no need to get up."

"Come to think of it," Mr. T. reached for his cane leaning against the porch rail, "I better get myself on up, like it or not. I need to get the three of us some tea, and an apple or two." He started to push himself out of the rocker. "It won't be a fittin' visit without a little refreshment."

"No, no," CeeGee touched his shoulder. "Mr. T., you stay here, I know where everything is. I'll be right back." CeeGee went in through the screen door and Elby leaned against the porch rail and started stroking Spunk the cat who was stretched out flat on top of it.

"Well, young man, Celia Gene tells me you go to private school on the mainland. How's that?"

"It's okay, I mean the classes are small and we all get a lot of attention. But since I have to travel back and forth all the time, I haven't really been able to get to know any kids around here. CeeGee is the only one."

"Well, she's a darn good start."

"Yes, sir, she is. I'd like to have my parents meet CeeGee, and maybe even Mrs. Williamson, since she is a teacher. I'm hoping maybe then I can come to school here on the island."

"We'll have our fingers crossed on that, Mr. Elby. And I hear our mutual friend has also spilled the beans with you about her Knowings and all. What do you think about that?"

"I hardly know what to think, it is something I've never heard of before in my whole life. She says that you help her do her best with all the things she knows, and I'd like to be a help to her, too, but I'm just a boy. I'm glad she has you."

"Well, young sir, I'm thinkin' you are a pretty special boy and our Celia Gene says the same. So now, like it or not, you have me, too."

"That's nice of you to say, sir. That makes two friends on the island. You know with her Knowings, I especially wonder about Ronnie Sampson…"

Just then, Cee Gee pushed open the screen door with her hip and carried out a tray with their tea and glasses, two apples and the peeling knife. "Yeah, Mr. T., just today Ronnie told me he's going to start drawing birds because he was so inspired by the John James Audubon book. And Miss McGuire is going to take him some more art books, and maybe some brownies, too."

"My land, child. You've been busy. You are workin' your magic, Celia Gene. I must say you are. So, you're tellin' me that crotchety old librarian is going to do somethin' nice for somebody?"

CeeGee set the tray down on the table. "She is. I had a Knowing that Miss McGuire's knight is never going to come, but someone else is, someone real and someone she would never have thought to dream about. She can have a whole different life if she reaches out to real people in a kind and generous way, instead of sitting around complaining and waiting for that knight to come to her." CeeGee poured a glass of tea and handed one to Mr. T. "So we talked about her useless knight, and then how she wants to fix up the library for the kids and teens, and how she doesn't have the money, but I told her that maybe if more people felt connected to the library there could be someone out there who would help out. So, she is going to do Books and Brownies, every week, for all the people in Southport who can't get in so easy, like Ronnie, and like Ernest Hughes and the people at the senior center and all." CeeGee was out of breath, so she stopped and poured a glass of tea for Elby and herself.

"My, my, my, since I last saw you, you've just reached up and tossed a whole new string of stars into the heavens. We're going to have a few new constellations before you're done, Missy. That's for darned sure."

CeeGee smiled and started to speak, but stopped herself from telling Mr. T. just yet that he was also on Miss McGuire's Books and Brownies list. CeeGee knew the librarian wasn't Mr. Tindale's favorite person on the island. She'd best let that part just play out on its own. "That's a real nice way to think of it, new stars in the heavens. Thank you, Mr. T."

"You know, Celia Gene, this talk of Audubon and all the books makes me think of my dear Maggie May. She used to love to go out on the marsh and sketch the birds out there. She'd spend all day watching them, and I'd spend all day watching her. We'd go down to the end of the boardwalk, and she'd take along a portable easel that she would set up, right in the middle of the glory of that place. I'd sit on the bench, down a ways, so she could concentrate. When she was all done, she'd come over and share her picture with me and tell me all about that bird, or turtle, or little mud hen. She saw the beauty in all of 'em. She'd come home and make a painting from those drawings. You seen 'em inside here, right child?" He rocked back and forth a few times as his memories wafted by.

"Yes, sir, I have, and they are beautiful," CeeGee answered.

"Elby son, just so's you know, Maggie May is my dear departed wife, and I miss her every day. You know, I still have all her drawing pens and pencils and her watercolor sets. She had brushes of every size and shape, and jars and tubes of paint in every color. Special papers, too."

"Oh my gosh," CeeGee remembered her conversation with Ronnie, "do you think…?"

Mr. Tindale interrupted, "Hey, Celia Gene, you think your Ronnie would like to have those artist things? I sure ain't using them and ain't never gonna."

"Oh my gosh, yes! That would be so perfect. Ronnie would love that!"

"I wish Ronnie could go see the bird sanctuary at the marsh for himself," Elby added. "Can you imagine how it would be for him to see all those different birds alive and moving, instead of just in books, or that one bird up in that one tree by his carport?"

"Yeah, but Ronnie doesn't get out much, you know. Actually, he doesn't get out at all," CeeGee said sadly.

Elby started to think out loud, and CeeGee could see his mind working even faster than his mouth. "You know, CeeGee, if we're right about your Knowing, and Ronnie really is going to graduate from high school and go off to art school…then, he's going to have to find a way to get out in the world a little, get comfortable somewhere besides home. He's not going to change years of isolation in a heartbeat."

Mr. T. sat up a little straighter in his chair. "Simple deductive reasoning. That's right, Mister Elby. Come to think of it…"

Elby finished the sentence for him. "The bird sanctuary at the marsh would be the perfect place to start." Elby smiled at him as he went on, "A nice, quiet place for someone to go and make art, even someone in a wheelchair. Especially someone who is shy and who's been cooped up a long time and wouldn't want to be around a lot of people and noise."

"That's right, and I remember that when they made the sanctuary at the marsh, they made it so people in wheelchairs could get in and out easy. I always thought it was nice they did that," CeeGee said, "but I've never seen anyone out there in a wheelchair before."

"Well, it's about time. So, do you think maybe we could take him?" Elby asked.

Mr. Tindale sat up even straighter. "Well, let's stew on this. I'm pretty sure there's room for his wheelchair in my car's big old trunk. We could just load up the chair, and the four of us, and off we go. You two would have to help out both me and Ronnie, he ain't the only one in this party that has a hard time gettin' around. Think you could do that?"

"That's no problem; we can do that." CeeGee said.

"Right, we'll help out both of you."

"You really think you can? I'm a pretty hefty guy, but I don't need that much help. How 'bout Ronnie, Celia Gene? I haven't seen the kid in years."

"Skinny as a rail."

"So then, why not? Together we should be able to lift him and get him in the car." Elby looked at CeeGee and she looked at Mr. T, and they all smiled at each other.

They decided they wouldn't be able to go to the sanctuary for at least a week because they figured it would take that long to get ready. First, Elby and CeeGee had to go to the senior center and get the folks who took care of the old people to teach them how to get a person safely out of a wheelchair and into a car, and back again. That took four lessons. After she and Elby got done at the senior center, CeeGee had to go to Ronnie's house to try to talk him into going along with their idea.

Ronnie had more excuses than she could count. He liked being at his house. He felt safe at his house. He liked his carport. He was happy looking at books. He didn't have to go somewhere to see real live birds. CeeGee and Elby were just kids. They weren't strong enough to lift him into a car. What if the car broke down? What if the boardwalk wasn't safe? What if he fell in the marsh? Who would be able to save him?

Finally, after telling Mr. Tindale about all of Ronnie's arguments and talking it over, CeeGee brought Ronnie a big pad of drawing paper and a set of colored pencils from Maggie May's art supplies. "Ronnie, I am not going to argue with you about this until it is time for me to go off to college. Look at these drawing pencils and this tablet. We also have a stand you can set up right in front of your chair to put the tablet on. It has a little shelf to hold all the pencils. If you come to the bird sanctuary with us, these art supplies will all be yours. To keep."

Ronnie took the tablets and the pencils from her. He looked at each pencil and touched the sheets of heavy paper in the tablet. Then he set them on his table under the target with the knives sticking out of it. He gave CeeGee another long look, as if he were sizing up her strength to lift him out of his chair.

Before he could say no again, CeeGee went on, "And just so you know, my friend Elby Smith is going with us too, and between the two of us we can get you into Mr. Tindale's big boat of a car. We took lessons."

"Okay, okay, but…"

"And besides that, I am telling you the truth about what you might see; look at this." She handed him the *Guide to the Birds on Magdalena Island* that she'd picked up from the library. It had been published by the parks department and had all the names and descriptions of island birds, as well as a photo of each. "See all the bird names that have SP by them," CeeGee said, "those are the birds that come in the spring, so some of them might still be there. And all the ones with an S by them are the ones that come in the summer, so they should be out there, too. And there are plenty that live here all year round, like the herons and the egrets and the ibises and gulls and terns. You know how many different birds you might see, including the uncommon and rare ones?"

"How many?"

"A couple dozen. I counted."

"Come on."

"I am not kidding."

Ronnie paged through the booklet, then looked back to the table with the tablets and pencils.

"You don't get the art supplies unless you come to the marsh," CeeGee reminded him.

"Well, heck," he finally said. "If this is the only way I'm gonna get my hands on those tablets and pencils, I give up."

Chapter Fourteen

When CeeGee finally got home that day, she trudged up the stairs from the carport, exhausted. On top of riding her bike all over town—from Mr. T's, to the library, and of course to the Triple S for some much-needed ice cream, and then back home every day— she'd had to do the wheelchair training at the Senior Center and ride over to Ronnie's for the everlasting arguments about the marsh. She felt like she was working as hard as her mom and her dad combined. Just as she got to the top of the stairs, she overheard her parents talking in the kitchen. She stayed out on the landing and listened.

"Carl Williamson, how many times do I have to ask? Can't you please just fix that teeny, tiny leak under the sink?"

"I work hard all day, Bobbie. I don't want to come home and work some more."

CeeGee knew instantly that her father had made a very big mistake.

"Oh really? You poor dear. And what do you think I do? Here's what I do. I teach summer school English to struggling high schoolers, then I come home and grade their highly flawed papers, and after that I cook dinner—for you. Would you like to complain some more, Carl Williamson?"

"You could call a plumber."

"I could call a plumber? First off, Carl, *you* could call the plumber. Second, it's a leak. It's not brain surgery."

CeeGee could hear her dad groan as he dropped to the floor. "All right, Bobbie, all right."

"You know what, Carl, you may have an idea there. Now that we won't have to hire a plumber to fix that simple, tiny, itty bitty leak, we might want to hire a cook to make dinner five nights a week. How does that sound, darlin'?"

CeeGee could hear her father's muffled voice from under the sink. "I'm doing it, Bobbie, okay? I'm doing it."

CeeGee waited until she heard her mother walk away, then let herself in quietly, stepped over her dad's legs and went to her room and collapsed onto her bed. Soon the smell of fried chicken drifted down the hall to her bedroom and Bobbie called the family to dinner.

CeeGee's family used to eat in the living room at a creaky old table they inherited from Bobbie's grandmother, but when Bobbie started teaching at the high school she needed a place to spread out her schoolwork and said she didn't want to have to clean it up every day, so the family could sit down and eat for ten minutes. Now the old table was her mother's office, covered with books and student papers, and the family ate at a new table in the kitchen.

Carl thought eating in the kitchen was a great idea. He had always hated that dining room table. He said the small chairs made him feel like he was at an elementary school parent-teacher conference. "Bossy teachers love to plant parents in those little dwarf chairs," he said, "just to get one up on them right off the bat." Every night when he had to fold himself into one of Bobbie's fancy chairs, he complained. "This chair was built for a midget."

"This was my grandmother's dining set, Carl," her mother always answered, as if that was all that needed to be said on the matter. As soon as Bobbie decided to move meals into the kitchen, Carl went out and bought the family a big, sturdy dining set. It was a little too big, but since there were only five of them, and the table could seat six, they pushed one narrow end against the kitchen wall and kept all the condiments down there.

The family came in and sat down to eat in their usual places— Carl at the head, Bobbie next to him on the side closest to the stove, CeeGee on her father's other side and the twins across from each other, as far away from their father as possible. The boys used to sit by their dad, until they were twelve and went from being the most wonderful boys in the whole, wide world according to their mother, to being total trouble magnets according to their father.

Bobbie served herself and passed the platter of fried chicken to Carl who took a breast and passed it on to CeeGee.

"So, I heard a juicy piece of gossip today," Bobbie said.

"And what would that be, Bobbie?" Carl asked.

"Guess."

"C'mon, Mom, at least give us a hint." Danny took the platter from CeeGee, picked out a thigh and pushed the platter across to his brother.

"It's about two young people."

"Gee, Mom, that narrows it down to half of Southport," Davey said. He put his elbow on the table, rested his chin in his hand, looked over at his brother and rolled his eyes. Danny did the exact same thing, the exact same way, at the exact same time.

"Yeah, could we at least know if it's about boys or girls?" Danny added.

"It's one of each."

"Bobbie, I fixed the blasted sink. Now will you please go ahead and tell your gossip without all of us having to arm wrestle you for it?"

"All right, here it is. Buster McCall has gone and given Alice Adams an actual engagement ring."

"What'd he go and do *that* for?" said Danny.

"Well, it's not surprising really. They've been going together for what, five years now?" Bobbie said.

"Right," said Davey, "and she has those great big…" as he began to raise his cupped hands to his chest, Bobbie swiped him a look. He dropped his hands quickly to his lap.

"Good, I hope now they will have someplace to go and play kissy face besides my soda shop."

Bobbie described the engagement ring and the plans for a fall wedding. She said neither of the parents were thrilled, but they were resigned. No one knew how those two teenagers were going to be able to support themselves on their own.

CeeGee was trying hard to listen to all this talk, when suddenly the light came into her. What was happening? She was at home! She had never had a Knowing about her family, and never, ever, ever did she have a Knowing in her own home. It was completely against her rules! What was this? Could she make it stop? But it was too late, the Knowing came. She didn't know how long she sat there with Buster and Alice's future playing out in her head, but when she came out of it, she heard her father say, "So, Celia Gene, tell us about that boy I've been seeing you with at the soda fountain the last few weeks."

Bobbie turned to look at her daughter. "Boy? Carl, you did not tell me about any boy."

Carl shrugged, "Guess I forgot."

"Forgot? About a *boy?*"

"It's okay, Mom, he, uh, he's my new friend." CeeGee answered, as she tried to stuff down the knowledge that had come to her in terrible waves.

"No way," Danny paused to lick chicken off his fingers. "CeeGee doesn't have friends."

"Danny, that's rude. Apologize to your sister. And, Carl, how could you forget to tell me about a BOY?"

"Sorry, sis."

Come on, Mom," Davey spooned more mashed potatoes onto his plate, "CeeGee's a loner. It's not a bad thing, just a fact. Right, sis?"

"Huh?" CeeGee felt naked, like she had accidentally taken off her clothes in public.

Bobbie held up a finger and pointed at each of the twins. "Not one more word from you two, hear me?" She turned to CeeGee and said sweetly, "So what's this boy's name, darlin'?"

"What?"

"Your new friend?" The whole family was waiting, staring at her.

"CeeGee, hello, his name?" Davey leaned toward his sister and waved a hand in front of her face.

"It's not going to be the way they think," CeeGee blurted out.

"The way who thinks?" Carl asked.

As if someone had pulled the plug from a sink full of water, CeeGee gushed on, "Alice and Buster. Alice is going to get really fat and Buster won't be able to hold down a job. He's never going to do anything more important than be the high school quarterback."

"Sounds right to me," Davey agreed.

"Yeah, the guy's an idiot," added Danny.

"How did we get back to Alice and Buster?" Carl said to Bobbie.

CeeGee pointed at her brothers. "Right!"

"Celia Gene, what in heaven's name are you talking about?" Carl asked.

CeeGee brought both hands to her cheeks. "And babies," she went on, shaking her head. "They're going to have too many babies."

"Yeah, well that sounds right, too," Carl said. "Davey, pass the potatoes."

"Please, all of you, hush," Bobbie ordered. She leaned across the table and looked at her daughter closely. "Celia Gene, are you all right? You look pale." She reached out to touch CeeGee's forehead.

CeeGee winced. "I don't, I…can I be excused? I don't feel good."

"Here, let me come with you." Bobbie started to push back her chair, but CeeGee waved her away and left the room in a rush.

CeeGee went to her bedroom, closed the door and sat down on the bed. She had broken her most important rule. She'd let a Knowing come into her house, into the circle of her family. She'd ruined everything for sure. She could see it. Her parents were sure to figure out what just happened, and then they would go back to the way they were when she was in third grade, angry and silent. What should she do? Everything was going so well, and now this. Her first thought was to go to Mr. Tindale for help, but he would think this was good. He wanted her to share her gift with her parents. He'd be glad this had happened.

Elby. Maybe she could talk to Elby. He was so smart. But his parents were in on his gift, so he might agree with Mr. T. Besides, she'd only just met him. If she was just one big problem, he might not want to be her friend anymore.

Then her thoughts jumped to Alice and Buster. Nothing in her Guide for Giving would help her out with this one, not that she could see. Alice and Buster would never listen to her, and even if they did, they'd be mad as two wet cats. And how was she going to share her Knowing in a kind and generous way? No one would want to hear this news in any way at all. She sure wouldn't want anyone telling her she was about to make the biggest mistake of her life and not one single thing was going to turn out the way she thought.

"Hey darlin'," Bobbie stuck her head through the doorway, "mind if I come in?"

"I'm tired, Momma."

"I know, dear, so am I. Just for a minute." Bobbie came in and sat on the side of the bed. She reached out and pushed a strand of hair behind CeeGee's ear.

The familiar gesture made CeeGee miss her and the time they used to spend together after school, at the kitchen table, drinking Dr. Peppers, talking about books and lessons and anything at all. That closeness seemed like a lifetime ago.

As if she was reading her mind, Bobbie said, "Celia Gene, I've been thinking about how we used to sit and talk after school. You know with a couple Dr. Peppers and some chips and salsa. And how lately, you've been so busy, and my work and the twins are always so demanding; seems like we get no time together at all. I've been missing you."

"Thanks, Momma," CeeGee said. Her mother had always seemed like a mind reader to her. The twins never got away with anything for long, because Bobbie could sniff out trouble like it was a storm coming. By the time CeeGee got old enough to do anything bad, she knew better.

"Besides, I'm dying to hear about this boy."

"I was going to tell you about him, Momma, but I've just been so busy and tired."

"Are you feeling all right now, darlin'?"

"Yeah, I'm okay. My new friend is named Elby, Elby Smith."

"Elby, now that's an interesting name. Tell me about this Elby." Bobbie turned sideways, lifted her feet up on the bed and plumped up a pillow behind her back. She leaned against the headboard and waited.

Before CeeGee told her mother about Elby, she decided she'd better explain the business with Alice and Buster at the dinner table and searched her mind frantically for a plan. "Momma, you know all that stuff I said about Alice and Buster? I guess, well, I think maybe I sounded pretty crazy, huh?"

"I've never thought you were crazy, Celia Gene, just very special. You are all I've ever dreamed of in a daughter."

Dreamed, dream—perfect. CeeGee landed on it and went, "You see, I'd already heard Alice and Buster were getting married, yesterday at school, I think. Someone said something about it, and then I had a dream about them last night. I forgot all about that dream at first, but then when you started talking about them it came back and it seemed like it was real, instead of a dream. You know how that can happen?"

"Really, why do you think you had a dream about the two of them?" Bobbie turned on her side to face her daughter.

"Well, you know, I see them down at the Triple S all the time pawing at each other, so maybe they just got stuck in my head, you know. And then they popped up in a dream after I went to sleep. Maybe that was it."

"That could be." Bobbie waited for CeeGee to go on as they sat in silence for a moment. "So, why don't you tell me whatever else you want to about your dream, and then we can talk about Elby."

"Oh, there wasn't much else, Momma, just what I said at dinner, that's all. It's kind of sad. They are so crazy about each other, but once they get married…well, it seems like it might just turn into a bad crazy, not a good crazy."

"You might not be too far off." Bobbie rolled onto her back and folded her hands across her stomach. "I wouldn't be surprised if Alice and Buster did turn out like you say. They're awfully young to marry. They are obviously very emotional, and they come from quite different families. But people grow up and change and so can they. It's their choice in the end." CeeGee half expected her to say Guide for Giving Number Five, but Bobbie went on, "Now, tell me about your new friend, Elby."

CeeGee told her mother how smart Elby was and how he went to school on the mainland, but he was hoping his parents would let him stay on the island next year. She said it felt like he was her first real friend her own age. Bobbie asked her questions until the subject of Elby was worn out. Then they talked about *To Kill a Mockingbird* for a while and how Scout was CeeGee's favorite book character so far. CeeGee told her mother about Books and Brownies and that Miss McGuire might actually do something nice for other people.

"Momma," CeeGee said, just as Bobbie rose to leave. "Can I talk to you about one more thing?"

"Sure, darlin', what is it?"

"I've been thinking. Remember Ronnie Sampson?"

"Why of course, who could forget that poor boy?" Bobbie sat back down at the edge of the bed, listening.

"Well, you know how we've all been talking about what Buster and Alice are going to do and how it might be hard and even if it is, they could change and make it better someday? But nobody talks about Ronnie anymore, and how hard his life might be, or how maybe it could be better."

"Well, that's true, but as far as I know, Ronnie doesn't talk to anyone else either."

"Well, I was thinking…"

"Yes, dear, go on," Bobbie prompted.

"Well…" CeeGee took a breath, "Well, it's just that I feel bad for him, stuck in that wheelchair, when I'm so lucky—able to walk to school and run on the beach and all."

Bobbie reached out and touched her arm. "Yes, and…"

"So, I was just wondering, why isn't Ronnie still in school?"

"Well, he's old enough to legally drop out, and I think it's safe to say that he has."

"Do you know if anyone at the school ever contacted him about finishing? You told me his mother doesn't take very close care of him."

"I don't know, Celia Gene. The boy was doing his best to drop out even before the accident."

"But, I remember you told me, he used to go to art class." CeeGee pressed.

"Yes, that's true. Ronnie did show up at school for art class. He was so good at it, but as soon as that one class let out, he'd scamper out of the building like a squirrel up a tree." Bobbie smiled at the memory, "Celia Gene, why the sudden interest in Ronnie Sampson?"

"I just feel bad for him. I went by his house one day, accidentally, and he was out on the carport. And even though he still looked scary and mean, I thought he seemed lonely. And I bet he's really sad about his future. It seems like the school should try to help him out. I mean, he has all this time and he's not causing trouble anymore. And Ronnie's not stupid, is he? At least he could finish high school."

Bobbie looked at her daughter hard, and CeeGee could tell she was debating between reprimanding her for going by Ronnie Sampson's house and praising her for being caring. CeeGee watched her mother's face and thought, *Please, please, please.*

"Well," Bobbie reached out to touch her daughter's cheek, "I could check into it, darlin'. Maybe I could get a guidance counselor to go over there and talk to him. If he's willing to try, I think we could send a tutor over to his house, or he could even come to the school. It's not far, he could probably make it there on his own. He wouldn't have to take all the classes, just enough to pass the test showing his competence. And you're absolutely right—Ronnie was never stupid, just wild."

"I bet he could catch up in no time," CeeGee carried on with enthusiasm. "And then, wouldn't it be great if after he graduates he could study some more, like go on to an art school or something? Get away from his crummy house, and the bad memories of his awful friends, and the accident."

"It seems like you've given this a lot of thought." Bobbie looked at her daughter tenderly. "I'm proud of you, Celia Gene." Bobbie thought a moment, then went on, "Tell you what—I'll get the guidance counselor to take some art school brochures with her when she goes over there. Maybe she could convince Ronnie that finishing high school would take him in a direction he'd really like to go. If he works hard, with his injuries and background, we might even be able to help him find a scholarship."

"Oh, Mom, that would be so great! I mean, a really, really bad thing might turn out to be good for him—in a way."

Bobbie raised her hand to her daughter, and CeeGee clasped it. "Here's to a chance for Ronnie to have a better future."

"A silver lining, something to hope for, Momma."

Chapter Fifteen

CeeGee rose from her bed, stuck her head out the window, saw the puffy clouds floating by and sniffed the air. Rain. She went outside in her pajamas and could see tiny, shining puddles on the ground. A summer rain must have swept over the island during the night and caused the heat to lift a little. The breeze was cool and moist, as if it was blowing into Southport from a faraway, perfumed country. The sky above her looked like a giant had tossed handfuls of enormous cotton balls into a see-through blue sky, and birds were skittering back and forth overhead as if they'd suddenly discovered it was just plain fun to fly.

It was the perfect day to go to the marsh. She had been so busy with Elby and Mr. Tindale and Ronnie, she hadn't been to the marsh in forever. She missed it and now they would all go together for a visit. On the weekends, the marsh was crowded with summer tourists, which wouldn't be good for Ronnie, and since CeeGee didn't like to be around crowds either, they decided late afternoon on a weekday was the best time to go. They had planned the trip for when the shadows began to grow long, and most visitors would have left. They knew the birds would still be there, especially the ducks.

Magdalena Island had always been known as a gathering place for all kinds of birds—local, migratory, rare and common. But the boardwalk at the marsh was still pretty new to Southport and was made to offer protection to these island treasures. Locals know from childhood that the brackish shore of a marsh is a sticky, gooey mess and completely off limits, but every year there'd be a few tourists who would wade into the muck, slogging right past the signs telling them not to. Seemed like they all wanted to have their picture taken next to a bird, or pet a bird, or do some other foolish thing involving a bird. They'd trample the marsh plants, get themselves stuck and sometimes sink in so deep the firemen had to come out and rescue them, which made the mess even worse.

So, in defense of the marsh, the citizens of Southport raised some money and had the city workers build a boardwalk that ran a few feet above the water all along the shoreline. There was a parking lot at the entry, and a wooden path that led to the boardwalk. At the trail head there was a box on a post filled with free brochures that showed the names and pictures of all the birds that people might see, with a check box by each one. They built a tower with a platform on top down at the very end of the boardwalk, so people could climb up for a panoramic view. The platform had two telescopes, one high enough for grownups and one with a step up for children. Now, the tourists stayed on the boardwalk like they were supposed to and instead of getting into trouble in the mud, they spent the whole day with the list, watching for the orioles, cormorants, herons and egrets. When they spotted one, they marked the box next to the bird's picture as if checking off a bird box was the whole point of being in such a magical place.

CeeGee went back inside, got dressed, ate some toast and peanut butter, then went to the living room and read over yesterday's paper. She went down to the backyard and sat on the swing until the rising heat and the bugs started to drive her crazy. She went back inside, read a little from the new book on Miss McGuire's list, *Moby Dick* by Herman Melville, which looked like it was going to be both hard and long. She fixed herself a sandwich around lunchtime, even though she wasn't really hungry, then looked at her watch. It felt like the longest day in history and there was still a few hours before it was time to go to Mr. Tindale's. She decided to go over to the Triple S and read some magazines off the rack.

Just as she had gotten herself settled in at the counter with a stack of magazines and a hot fudge sundae from Johnny, she heard noises behind her. She lifted her head to listen and could tell right away that Buster and Alice had come in and were in one of the booths making their usual sickening smooching sounds. She didn't think she could stand it one more minute. She spun around on the bar stool until she saw them, sitting on the same side of the booth, laced up against each other like two vines. She spun back to the counter. What to do? She had a Knowing to share. And she had to be kind with it. Maybe if she spun around a few times it would clear her head, but with every spin, Buster and Alice passed in front of her eyes and she just got more confused. Think, think, think. She kept on spinning and soon fell into a dream-like state that emptied her head, making room for an idea to come in that could help her do what she had to do. By about the fiftieth spin, and feeling so dreamy she was about to fall off the stool, she had her idea. A dream. How obvious! It had worked with her mother, why not with the two of them?

She slid off the stool and staggered over to Buster and Alice. She had to clear her throat three times before they looked up.

"What?" Buster said.

"I hear you two are planning to get married. That right?" CeeGee stood before them, weaving slightly.

"None of your business." Buster tried to wave CeeGee off, but Alice unwound herself and held up her left hand to show the tiny diamond chip on her engagement ring.

"Hey, that's real nice, Alice. Congratulations."

"Get lost." Buster said.

"Just give me a minute, okay?" CeeGee said to Buster. "Listen, I don't even know y'all that well, but it's a funny thing, after I heard you were getting married, I had a dream about the two of you. I thought maybe you'd want to know about it."

"Not interested."

"Buster, let her tell. It'll be fun." Alice turned sideways on the bench, hugged her knees and looked up at CeeGee with anticipation all over her perky cheerleader face. "What did you dream?"

"Well, it was pretty confusing to me, but I've heard people say that dreams have a special meaning, so maybe you can figure it out." CeeGee tried to look innocent like Danny and Davey would do with their mother. "Anyway, in my dream you were married, like you're planning, right?"

"That's right, at Thanksgiving."

"So, in my dream, it was a while later because you were already married, but it was funny because Buster wasn't around much. He was always off with the guys or something."

"Why, Buster honey," Alice turned back to him and said in a sing-song voice, "you wouldn't leave me all alone for a bunch of messy old boys. Now would you?" She tugged at a button on his shirt.

"No, baby, I only want to be with you." He leaned over and stuck his tongue in her ear.

CeeGee felt like she might throw up but forced herself to go on. "And you had a bunch of babies—seemed like they came right away and real close to each other. My mom had twins before me and she talks about how much work that was for her when we were all little."

Alice sat up straight, "How many babies?"

"Lots. I couldn't even count them all. Oh, and Alice, these big muscles you're so crazy about," CeeGee reached out and poked at Buster's bicep. "He didn't have those anymore, he had this." CeeGee puffed out her cheeks, arched her back and pointed at her stomach.

"Hey, kid, you watch what you're saying." Buster pushed on Alice's shoulder and tried to get out of the booth, but she pushed him back without taking her eyes off CeeGee. "Baby, don't listen to this," he said.

Alice looked down at her shoulder, then at Buster, then began straightening her skirt and blouse.

"Come on, this kid doesn't know anything. It's just a stupid dream," Buster said.

CeeGee rushed on, "But wait, I remember now, it wasn't so great for you either, Buster. You had a hard time holding down a job, and after a while Alice got discouraged and spent the whole day in her robe and slippers. And she ate a lot—a whole lot. And the house was a big mess. And she never wanted to…well, you know… make any more babies." CeeGee paused to let that sink in. "So, I thought maybe you'd want to know. Maybe you two can figure out what it all means. Beats me." CeeGee smiled at them and shrugged.

Alice and Buster sat frozen, staring back at her, their minds taking in all that CeeGee had told them. Finally, Buster took a firm hold of Alice's arm. "Let's get one thing straight, Alice, there ain't going to be no robe and slippers when I get home from work."

"That's *if* you go to work, you mean." Alice jerked her arm away. "And I'm telling you right now, I do *not* want a whole mess of kids. You hear me?"

Buster got right in her face. "Fine, then you'll have lots of time for cooking."

"You better watch it, Buster." Alice poked at his chest.

CeeGee figured she'd better get out of there before they decided to be mad at her instead of each other. She turned away quietly and went back to the counter to put the magazines away, but paused when she heard Alice say, "Well, how many kids are you thinking, Buster? This is something we ought to decide *before* we get married, don't you think?"

"I don't know—a few, a bunch, I like kids. A team, I guess?"

"A team? What kind of team? Basketball, bobsledding? I mean, teams come in a lot of sizes, Buster."

"Well, a good-sized team, I'd say. Wouldn't you?" Buster added earnestly, "Football, maybe?"

"Football? Do you seriously think I am going to give birth to an entire football team? Are you *crazy?*"

CeeGee quickly left the store, trying not to laugh out loud and attract their attention. Then she checked in her mind to see if she had followed any steps on her guide at all. She didn't know how she could have told them about their future in a kind and generous way, or how she would want to be told, as she had no intention of getting married while she was still a teenager. And she couldn't imagine needing to have anyone tell her what a bad idea that was. As far as looking for silver linings, well, hopefully something might show up later, but she sure didn't see anything at the moment. And she didn't really tell them that they could change their direction and change their future, but that's exactly what they were talking about right now, so maybe she had opened a door. All in all, not so great, except that Buster and Alice got a chance to start looking at where they were headed, instead of just trying to get there as fast as they could.

CeeGee took off on her bike and by the time she arrived at Mr. Tindale's, Elby was already there. Mr. T. had pulled the car out of the garage and they were checking to make sure the trunk was clean and empty. She let go of her brooding about Buster and Alice and joined the team. CeeGee and Elby spent some time practicing what they had learned at the senior center and showing Mr. T. how they would lift Ronnie into the car. Mr. Tindale watched from the sidelines and coached them.

"A little higher now." He gestured up with the palm of his hand. "I think you need one more step to the right, Celia Gene."

He waved her to the right. "Easy now, Elby, be sure to let him down nice and easy. That looks fine, just fine."

Finally, they all got in the car and drove over to Ronnie's house. Even though they were a little early, he was there, anxiously waiting for them under the shade of the carport. Mr. T. pulled into Ronnie's driveway and stopped. CeeGee and Elby got out of the back and opened the car door to the front passenger side. Then they wheeled Ronnie over and turned him, so he was facing front, the same direction as the car. CeeGee got on one side of him and Elby on the other and they leaned down toward Ronnie and asked him to put an arm around each of their shoulders.

"You two sure you know what you're doin'? Ronnie asked.

"We got this, Ronnie." Elby answered.

CeeGee and Elby scooted their hands under Ronnie's legs, between the knee and his behind. "One, two, three," CeeGee counted and said, "Hold on, Ronnie." He tightened his grip around their shoulders and together they lifted Ronnie up. Mr. T. helped them out by pulling the wheelchair back and away. Then they took two or three small, shuffling steps to turn Ronnie sideways, so his back was to the seat of the car.

"One, two three," Elby said, and they took two more steps closer to the car and set Ronnie down gently, pulling their hands from under his legs as they carefully lowered him onto the car seat.

CeeGee said, "Ronnie, can you reach over and grab the dashboard and help us out?" Ronnie twisted to his left and took hold of the dashboard with both hands. CeeGee lifted his legs and shifted them into the car. Elby stayed by Ronnie's back side to make sure he stayed on the seat, and the rest of him swiveled around the same as his legs.

They stood back and watched Ronnie squirm a little, press his fists against the seat to lift himself up and get himself settled. "Hey, that wasn't half bad."

"Good work, you two," Mr. Tindale called out to them from behind the car where he was folding up Ronnie's chair to put it in the trunk. Elby went to the back of the car and helped load the wheelchair, then went and opened the driver's door for Mr. Tindale. Elby took his cane and stood by while Mr. T. settled himself into the driver's seat, then got in the back seat with the cane. CeeGee got in on the other side behind Ronnie. As they pulled out of the driveway, Elby was grinning and CeeGee was trying not to cry.

They drove across town toward the ferry landing, but before they got there they took a left and went past the community swimming pool and through the entrance gate to the bird sanctuary. Once they got to the parking area by the trail head, Mr. T. pulled into a shady spot where they could get the wheelchair, and then Ronnie, out of the car. Which they did, better than the first time. CeeGee pushed Ronnie's chair on to the wooden path and paused at the post for him to grab the bird list. Elby walked Mr. Tindale over to the path and stayed close by to make sure he didn't stumble on a loose board.

Elby and Mr. T. went on ahead, and CeeGee followed behind, pushing Ronnie's chair slowly down the path until they reached the sloping ramp up to the boardwalk. She pushed him up the ramp and the marsh came into view. She stopped to take it in and heard Ronnie's low whistle when he saw the wide pond, dotted with little grass-covered islands and a gentle breeze rippling the water. The late afternoon sun cast a sheen across the marsh and lit up the dragonflies that hovered above the water. Ronnie cocked his head and tried to look back over his right shoulder. CeeGee turned the chair around so he could see the shore side of the marsh and Ronnie leaned forward in his chair to look over the railing. They both stayed quiet. First, they heard the tiny pat-pat-pat of the weak surge washing in and out, licking at the algae on the muddy shore. Then there was a slight squishing sound as turtles and mud hens padded around the water's edge.

After a while, Ronnie nodded and CeeGee turned him back around and continued down the boardwalk, past Mr. T. who had settled himself on bench. They kept going until they arrived at a small turnout with another bench, a place where people could get off the walkway and sit and watch the wide expanse of water. CeeGee wheeled Ronnie in to the open space next to the bench and started to get the pencils and paper out of the bag on the back of the chair, but Ronnie raised a hand to stop her. CeeGee put the supplies down on the bench, went up to the guardrail and leaned against it. She breathed in the marsh, then breathed out all the busyness of the last weeks and breathed in the marsh again. She felt the breeze come up on her face and heard the cattails rustle against each other, which seemed to cue the songbirds deep in the brush to join in. She glanced back at Ronnie and he had his head cocked—he was listening too.

Soon, the whole marsh symphony began to play its soft and tender tune, layered with sounds that were completely different from the windy, booming bravado of the beach. CeeGee felt her spirit go calm and her mind go quiet. For her, this is what the marsh was—a place she could come to just be—to see, to hear and to feel. A rich entry to another place. Not a place to take pictures or check off bird names or even point at anything. Ronnie had tucked the bird list into the side of his chair and he seemed to want to be silent too. CeeGee looked back at Mr. T. on his bench and could almost see Maggie May sitting by his side, holding his hand, the two whispering together. Elby had gone all the way down to the platform at the far end and climbed to the top. He was looking through the telescope deep into the vast distance.

Ronnie looked so at peace. CeeGee settled on the bench next to his wheelchair, and they stayed that way for a long time, in silent admiration and awe. Soon a few herons landed, daintily lifting their long legs as they stepped through the shallows, their curved necks bent down to the water, watching for fish. Smaller ibis walked on their short stilts across the many little islands, getting lost in the grasses, then appearing again. The multi-colored ducks seemed to perform in front of the boardwalk, swimming around in circles, like ice skaters doing exercises in their fancy, flashy costumes of silver and purple, teal and cinnamon. Terns were posted like soldiers all over the marsh, all facing the same way, the black caps on the tops of their heads ruffled by the light breeze.

CeeGee looked over at Ronnie again. His usual suspicious gaze had melted into wonder, and she knew the marsh had filled his whole heart with its pure, sweet song. Just as it did hers.

Later, Mr. T. raised his hand and signaled it was time to leave. Dusk was coming and the shadows on the marsh were growing longer. She packed up the supplies and hung the bag on the back of Ronnie's chair. Just as she got ready to turn him around to leave, she caught a glimpse of color on the far side of the pond. Ronnie saw it too and reached up to touch her hand. There in the distance, a tall Roseate Spoonbill swooped down from the sky, stuck its long legs out in front as it aimed for the shallows and splashed into a light landing. The giant bird steadied and turned its head this way and that to survey the marsh. After a few moments, the spoonbill crouched slightly, leapt out of the water and lifted its wings into flight. It looked like a ballerina, with its neck stretched out, wings spread wide and its delicate, spindly legs pointed back, skimming the water. Its feathers were a tender shade of pink, and the little scooped out spoon at the tip of its bill looked like an artist had spilled a blob of darker pink on an otherwise perfect painting.

CeeGee's eyes went past the soaring spoonbill to the far horizon where a melon sun was beginning to drop beneath stringy clouds. As the light softened to the pale, muted shades of evening, the long shadows of the reeds painted gray lines on the surface of the water. CeeGee took a deep breath and knelt beside Ronnie. "Do you want me to get the paper and pens so you can draw that bird, Ronnie?"

"I don't need to draw it. I mean, I don't need to draw it now, because I will never, ever forget it." He looked directly at CeeGee and smiled with a sweetness in his face that she had never seen before. "I will never forget a single thing I saw today."

Elby ran past her and squeezed her shoulder as he went to help Mr. Tindale. He offered out his arm like Mr. T. was royalty. "Why, Elby sir, I think you might be the kindest young man I have ever met. Thank you for your assistance today."

"It is my complete pleasure, sir."

When they got to the end of the boardwalk, they all paused and turned back for one last look.

Mr. Tindale sighed and said, "I think this might be the best day I have had since my dear Maggie May left this earth."

"Did you feel her nearby today, Mr. T.?" CeeGee asked.

"I did, in a soft sort of way. She doesn't seem so far away these days." He looked at each of them with kindness in his eyes. "You know, I can hardly get out and around much anymore. And the three of you, well, you gave me a big gift. I want to say thank you, sure enough."

Ronnie cleared his throat. "Me, too. I want to say thank you, too. To all of you. Sorry I made it so hard to get me here. If we ever have a chance to do this again, I won't be such an ass."

They all drove in silence to Ronnie's house, unloaded him and his chair and one by one said goodbye. Elby and Mr. T. patted Ronnie on the shoulder, but CeeGee leaned down and hugged his neck.

On the way back to Mr. Tindale's, CeeGee told them that her mother was going to send a guidance counselor over to Ronnie's house to talk to him about finishing high school. The news was like the perfect punctuation mark at the end of a perfect sentence.

But when the moment came to also tell them she had a Knowing about Buster and Alice at her family dinner table, and that she had covered up the Knowing with her mother as if it came to her in a dream, and then did it again when giving the Knowing to Buster and Alice, she couldn't bring herself to tell them this at all. She wasn't sure why. Was she afraid they would judge or criticize when they never had before? Or did she just feel more independent somehow, since the Knowing came and got delivered all in the space of a day, and all on her own? Or was it more about her family? Did this Knowing, since it happened at home, somehow belong to her and her family? That was an idea that went against everything she had ever believed about her gift. She felt like she needed a map of the stars again, so she could find her way from constellation to constellation without getting so lost.

Chapter Sixteen

CeeGee sat in the library, waiting for Elby while updating her new calendar and to-do list that she got from the office supply aisle at the Triple S. After the day they took Ronnie to the marsh, it seemed like the peaceful mood they all shared just evaporated for CeeGee. Now it was day after day of trying to keep up with her Knowings and figuring out the ways to help people find the best future they could for themselves. It was getting to be too many people and too long a list for her. CeeGee just couldn't keep everything in her head anymore. But as she looked over her list, she was relieved to see there were a few items she thought she could cross off.

Just last week, the high school guidance counselor had gone to Ronnie Sampson's house to meet with him. CeeGee and Bobbie had planned about thirteen arguments the counselor could use to talk Ronnie into the idea of finishing high school, expecting him to be as stubborn about this as he'd been about going to the marsh. The guidance counselor was prepared to tell him that a tutor would come to his house, or that a special van could pick him up and bring him to the school, or that he could come on his own, and that he could take as long as he needed with his studies, and that other young men in Southport had done what they were suggesting for him, or any combination of those arguments. They'd even given the counselor pictures to take to Ronnie to remind him of how everything at the school was built so he could get around in his wheelchair just fine.

After she met with Ronnie, the counselor told Bobbie that Ronnie agreed without any hesitation at all. No arguments had been needed as Ronnie's answer was an immediate 'yes'. Ronnie did ask the guidance counselor what he needed to do to help make this happen, and they agreed it would be a good idea to get a tutor for him as soon as possible. The counselor said if he worked hard over the summer, he might be able to catch up. He could be ready to enter high school in the fall prepared for a new school year, picking up where he had been before the accident.

CeeGee and Elby had both gone over to Ronnie's house to congratulate him on his decision. They told him they would be happy to help him get used to studying, and even help him prepare for his big final test when the time came. He immediately accepted their offers as well. The sweet expression on Ronnie's face that CeeGee had seen at the marsh had faded a little, but it was still there. She felt confident she could mark 'Get Ronnie to Agree to Graduate from High School' off her list.

The next two items were 'Help with Books and Brownies' and 'Help with Library Remodel'. CeeGee didn't know if there was anything she could do with these two, but since they were part of her Knowing about Miss McGuire, she had felt obliged to put them on her list. CeeGee felt like a complete failure in helping Miss McGuire's Knowing to come true, until the librarian told CeeGee her news. She said she had scheduled a meeting with the mayor of Southport in hopes that there was just a little bit of money in the city budget he could allocate for some improvements to the library. To her surprise, the mayor had said there was—just a little.

Miss McGuire had gone right to work planning and scheming how she could make every penny count, drawing all of her ideas on her big sheets of paper. Then she got herself all worked into a dither because she couldn't stretch the money far enough, no matter how many pencil erasers she used up.

That's when CeeGee told Miss McGuire that Mike Robins knew how to design, plan and build things—houses, porches, coffins, whatever—and suggested that she talk to him. Miss McGuire took CeeGee's suggestion and invited Mike to the library to see what he thought might be accomplished with the limited funds. Mike told her the first thing he could do was build two big bookcases that could be used as dividers to separate the spaces for the teens to study and the young children to have their story hour. He also suggested that she could paint the walls of those spaces in different colors, so people would know they were for separate uses. He calculated what improvements could be added later as more money became available and gave her an idea of the cost of each step in the project. After talking to Mike, Miss McGuire figured she had enough money for the two bookcases and the paint. And maybe, if she managed her spending carefully, she could even afford a few new tables and chairs.

When she told Mike about her plan, he said he might be able to make the tables himself, and he'd do it just for the cost of the materials because Rosa brought his kids over to the library for the children's story hour every week and he knew what it meant to them. For the chairs, he thought they might do better on the cost if they went to the mainland and got them second hand. He said he would also donate refinishing, if the chairs needed it.

Miss McGuire tried to be thankful, and said so to Mike, but she wanted so much more than this, like a big, new check-out counter and a conference room for groups on the island to have their meetings, and enough money to buy some nice art to display, so visitors to the library could see and learn from more than just books. Plus, she wanted even more tables and chairs, and more bookcases, and lots and lots of new books to fill up her new spaces. She kept hoping that if she kept on with Books and Brownies, and kept telling people about her plans, she might find someone who would want to donate the money, but so far no one had offered.

CeeGee's dad said Miss McGuire spent too many years saying she didn't need any help from anybody to expect someone to step up and offer it now. The librarian was in a dither all the time, trying to save money here so she could spend money there. She fussed so much, people in the library started shushing her instead of the other way around.

CeeGee left her list on the table and went over to say hello to Mike where he was measuring for the bookcases. She hadn't seen him since Mrs. Robins' funeral. The grief and trouble from losing his job and his wife all in the same year had added some lines to his face, but even so, he looked like a new man. His hair was cut nice and neat and his muscles showed through his t-shirt. He'd taken some string and blocked off the area where he and Miss McGuire thought the new bookcases should go and he was kneeling on the floor measuring everything exactly and laying out the design.

CeeGee stood by while he took a tape measure out of his carpenter's belt and pulled a stubby pencil from behind his ear. He began to make marks on the floor as he inched forward. CeeGee stayed quiet so he could hold the numbers in his head and finish his work, but pretty soon he looked up and saw her.

"Why, Celia Gene! How you be, girl?" He stood and looked like he wanted to give her a big hug, but thought better of it, and reached out and squeezed her shoulder.

"How are you, Mike? It's good to see you again."

"You know, Celia Gene, we're all doin' okay, thanks to the work I have coming in with Sandwith Brother's, and now here. And that Rosa Leon, I don't know how I'd manage without her help with the house and the kids." He lowered his voice and leaned over closer to her. "But, I have to tell you, Miss Celia Gene, it sure is easier to raise four kids and build custom coffins than it is to please our Miss McGuire over there." He jerked his head to the counter where Miss McGuire was sitting, busy with her pencil and ruler, going over the drawings, making sure everything was just the way she wanted it for the thousandth time.

CeeGee looked from Mike to the checkout counter and nodded, "She has a lot of opinions."

"That's for sure," Mike shook his head and ran his fingers through his hair. "Just when I think we finally got the plans all set, she comes bustling over telling me to do this, don't do that, change this other. I ain't never seen anything like it."

CeeGee looked back at the librarian and saw he was right, Miss McGuire looked tight as a tick. "Tell you what, I'll go talk to her, maybe I can help out."

"That would be much appreciated, Celia Gene, I can use all the help I can get with that lady. Whew-wee!"

CeeGee walked over to the counter and sat on the stool across from the librarian. "How's it going, Miss McGuire?"

"Not well, Celia Gene, not well at all. That Mike Robins is simply not absorbing my vision for this new library. I feel like I am talking to a stump. He just keeps saying we need to do it this way, can't do it that way. He will not listen to me and he does not seem to understand that I know exactly what I want. This is, after all, *my* library."

"He did a really good job on our screen porch a couple summers ago, and Mr. Tindale's casket."

"Yes, well, a screen porch and a casket are a far cry, wouldn't you agree, from a *public* library?"

CeeGee looked at the upside-down sketches for a while longer and then said, "You know, Mike's been building things for a lot of years. I wonder if maybe his ideas and opinions are coming from all that he's learned. You know, from his years of experience and all? Maybe it's kind of like your list of the 'Best Books by American Authors'."

"Well, the knowledge it took to make up my list did come from many, many years and a veritable wealth of experience, no doubt about that." Miss McGuire brushed a few more eraser bits from her plans.

"So, do you think maybe Mike Robins is like that too, far as building things goes?"

"Celia Gene, this is not his library. He has absolutely no experience with *my* library."

"That's true, but he does have experience with building special rooms in lots of buildings, and setting them out so they work right," CeeGee pushed.

"Oh, alright Celia Gene, I get your point." She rolled up the plans, put them under the counter and changed the subject. "So, enough talk about that insufferable Mike Robins. Where are you on my list?"

"Well, a while back I finished Harper Lee's, *To Kill a Mockingbird* and now I'm reading Herman Melville's *Moby Dick*."

"Is that all? That is not much progress, Celia Gene."

CeeGee quickly added, "I've been trying to get through *Portrait of a Lady*, for what seems like forever, but I don't like it much."

"And why is that, may I ask?"

"It is way, way, w-a-y too long."

"Well, many of literature's finest books are long, Celia Gene. You are just going to have to accept that these well-known authors know what they are doing. But I must add, this would indicate you are reading the books out of order, which as you know, I do not recommend."

CeeGee could tell Miss McGuire was getting ready to start tsk, tsk, tsking her, so she said quickly, "Sort of like how Mike Robins knows how to build things in order, you mean?"

"Oh, all right, all right, Celia Gene. As I have already said once before, I got your point. Now, I must finish my work here, and you must get back to your reading." Miss McGuire waved the air with her hand, shooing CeeGee away.

"Well, good luck, Miss McGuire. I'm predicting everything is going to turn out plumb perfect." The librarian harrumphed and CeeGee turned back toward her table. It seemed like Miss McGuire had a long way to go before her Books and Brownies were going to lead her to a generous heart, true love and a better life. But, like Mr. Tindale always said, things were not necessarily going to happen on CeeGee's schedule.

When she got back to the table, Elby was there looking over her calendar and to-do List. CeeGee felt her back go up a little, like Miss McGuire.

"I don't see Mr. Tindale on here," Elby said as he scanned the list once more.

"What about him?" CeeGee said as she took her papers off the table.

Elby held both hands up and sat down across from her. "I'm just saying that I don't see him on your calendar or your list. Have you been over to see him lately?"

"No, not for a while, I've been too busy."

"Really? Too busy for Mr. T.?"

CeeGee also sat down. "What do you mean by that?"

"I just mean…Mr. Tindale has been your friend for a long time, CeeGee." Elby went on, "Lord knows, people like you and me don't have many. He's an old man and he's all alone. I just think you should make sure you stay close to him."

CeeGee doodled in the margin of her list and said nothing for a moment, then asked, "Have *you* been to see him this week?"

"No, but I only know him because of you. You are first with him," Elby argued.

"Yeah, you're right." CeeGee said without looking up, "I know you're right."

"I'm not criticizing you." Elby leaned in closer. "It's just that I know he really cares about you. And I know you feel the same about him."

"You're right, I'll go soon." Now it was CeeGee's turn to change the subject. "Have you heard about Miss McGuire's list?"

"What list?"

CeeGee told him about 'Miss McGuire's Personal List of the Best Books by American Authors' and named all the ones she had read. Elby had already read most of them, of course, but he wanted to join in anyway. He would start where she was, and in his spare time backtrack and pick up any he'd missed.

"So, what are you reading now?" he asked.

"I keep trying to read Henry James' *Portrait of a Lady*, but it's nine thousand pages long and James spends about a thousand pages at a time describing a room, or a garden or every single detail of Miss Isabel Archer's dress."

"Sounds boring. Why'd Miss McGuire pick it?"

"You're asking me why Miss McGuire does anything? Ask her. She'll be happy to tell you. So, can you read James real fast and give me the short version? Then we can read *Moby Dick* together, it's pretty good."

"Sure, I'll do that," Elby said. They talked about books until Elby had to go home. CeeGee was relieved because he was acting like her best friend again, instead of an adult lecturing her on what to do.

Before he left, Elby asked, "Where do I get the list—from Miss McGuire?" CeeGee nodded and he said, "I'll get it and check out a few books before I leave. This'll be fun!"

CeeGee remembered another of Miss McGuire's rules and added, "Forget about reading Fitzgerald's *The Great Gatsby*, she won't let you."

"I already read all of Fitzgerald."

"That figures."

"Want to meet here tomorrow afternoon?"

"Sure, see you then."

CeeGee sat alone at the table thinking about what Elby had said. The way she felt about Mr. Tindale hadn't changed. She loved him. It was just that she was just getting so busy with her own life. That and, to be honest, she still didn't feel like she wanted to tell him about the Knowing she had at the dinner table about Buster and Alice and how their marriage was going to turn out so bad. She knew what he would say—that having a Knowing at home meant she should open up to her family. It proved they could be with her as she shared her gift. Maybe staying away from him had to do with not wanting to share that stubborn secret of hers.

But on top of that, she felt like she was growing up and could make decisions on her own better than when she first met him. Maybe she didn't need him the way she used to, and that's why she hadn't made time for him lately. The thought made her feel ashamed. She wasn't being kind and generous to the very person who taught her what being kind and generous really meant. Had she learned nothing?

Maybe she'd go over to his house today. No, after the library she had to go to the Shop and Save for her mother to pick up some things for dinner. She couldn't go see him after dinner either, by then it would be too late. She decided she would get up early in the morning and go see him first thing. Maybe they could fix some skillet oatmeal for breakfast. She'd make it, he'd like that.

She went over all the things she had to tell Mr. Tindale. There were so many, she had to start making a new list. First, she needed to tell him all about Ronnie going back to high school. He'd be proud of how CeeGee and her mom had helped out. Just like he said, her mom had been the best one to talk to about helping Ronnie graduate. And he'd like it that even though CeeGee and her Mom made a list of all the ways they could talk Ronnie into finishing high school, they didn't need to use a single one.

CeeGee figured Miss McGuire had been to Ronnie's house for Books and Brownies by now and wondered if he liked all the books on art, so she added going over to Ronnie's to chat with him to her list. Plus, she needed to find out if Ronnie had been brave enough to show his birds to Miss McGuire, and if so, what she thought of them.

Oh, and she'd have to be sure to update Mr. T. on how Mike's work was going at the library, and how hard it was for him working for such a bossy old grump. She could just hear Mr. Tindale saying, 'Well, maybe with Mike's good influence, that old bird will learn to be generous, so she can find true love someday.' After they talked, and had a nice breakfast, she'd get back to work on the garden. And then later, they could share some sweet tea and an apple. That's right. That's what she'd do. All of that.

Chapter Seventeen

The next morning, CeeGee rose to a brilliant day. As she left her house, the sky was still pink at the edges and stuffed full of animal-shaped clouds, the kind she liked to lie down in the grass and stare at all day. Every bird on Magdalena Island was out looking for breakfast, in the trees and overhead, on the roof ridges and the telephone lines, all of them making a big, noisy ruckus. The cool gulf breeze carried the smell of the sea—beached seaweed and shellfish.

As she rounded the corner to Mr. Tindale's house on her bike, she half expected to see him already sitting out on the porch in his creaky old rocker reading the paper, but he wasn't. She went up the walk and saw that the flowerbed was a sorry tangle of weeds and dead blossoms. That was her fault; later today, she'd clean things up and water. Maybe Elby could come over and help her do the gardening while Mr. Tindale talked to them from the porch.

The front door was closed so she banged on the screen a few times before she let herself in. Mr. Tindale never locked his door and wasn't afraid of being robbed, "What's a body got to lose at my age?" he always said. "If they think they need it so bad, let 'em take it."

She called out to him from the front room but got no answer. Then the chill entered her, ice cold and dark. She moved toward Mr. Tindale's bedroom through air that was blue and misty, and cold as a meat locker. The doorknob was a lump of ice in her hand.

She stepped into his room. On the bed, Mr. Tindale lay curled on his side, like a sleeping child. His hands were clasped together under his chin and his feet stuck out of the covers, pigeon-toed and crossed over each other.

CeeGee stopped to gaze at her dear friend. She had never seen him so still. She wanted to reach out and touch the white stubble of yesterday's beard on his cheeks and smooth down the fine wisps of his hair spread out on the pillow like a soft gray halo. She wanted to tell him how sorry she was to have been gone, and that she was back. And that she would never leave him all alone, ever again.

She reached out to touch his cheek, and time stopped.

CeeGee would never know how long she stood over him, frozen, but when time started up again, she had no feelings inside, only the thoughts of what she must do. She looked at the phone beside the bed and saw a sticker on it with a number to call—*In Case of Emergencies*. She called the number.

"Police Station," a voice said.

"My best friend has passed," CeeGee said.

"Just a minute... All right, tell me where you are."

"I'm at Mr. Tindale's house."

"Yes, we know the house. And you're sure? He isn't breathing?"

"He's gone."

"Who is this, please?"

"I'm Celia Gene, Celia Gene Williamson."

"You're just a child. Are you there alone?"

"Yes."

"We will come right away. I want you to hang up this phone and call your parents. Get someone to come be with you. Can you do that?"

"Yes," CeeGee said again. The phone buzzed in her ear like an insistent bee for some time before she noticed it, set it back in the cradle and looked around the room. Should she tidy up? Were the dishes done? Mr. Tindale wouldn't want anyone to come over and think he didn't know how to keep up his house. Then she remembered—Rosa. Of course, his house would look just fine, but she should check anyway just to make sure.

She went to the kitchen and saw the dishrag folded neatly over the edge of the sink and a towel on the hook beside it. The dish drainer was empty. She saw the kitchen phone sitting on the built-in desk and Mr. Tindale's bills stacked neatly on a narrow shelf above it. The yellow tablet he used to make all their notes and lists was on the desk also.

She remembered that the police had said she should call someone.

She called home and her mother answered. But when CeeGee tried to speak, her voice sounded like an echo bouncing around the cold tomb in which she stood. She couldn't understand her own words.

"Don't you move, baby. I'm coming. I'll be there in minutes," her mother said.

CeeGee sat down at the kitchen table where she and Mr. Tindale had spent so many hours together. She put her feet close together, folded her hands like a child in prayer and waited.

When Bobbie came through the front door and saw her daughter, she rushed to her, pulled her to her feet and held her tight. CeeGee offered no response at all, but Bobbie didn't release her until the ambulance arrived and she had to meet the medics at the front door. Mr. Tindale's house filled up with all these noisy strangers and their equipment. Two big men pushed a tall, rolling bed across the living room and into Mr. Tindale's bedroom. CeeGee remained standing in the kitchen, her arms hanging limp at her sides.

Bobbie came back and took CeeGee by the arm. "Baby, I'm taking you home." She guided her past Mr. Tindale's bedroom, past the medics and the gurney, through the front door, down the steps, past the bright yellow van. Bobbie sniffed the air and looked to the south where the horizon had swollen into a thick, gray band. The air was damp and heavy. The birds had gone silent and taken cover as a storm rolled across the gulf toward the island. Bobbie pulled her daughter tighter and CeeGee stumbled slightly and shivered as if it were freezing outside, the way it had been inside Mr. Tindale's house. "We'll come back for your bike later," her mother said.

Bobbie drove them home and parked in the carport. She came around to open the door for CeeGee, and they climbed the stairs to the kitchen. Once through the door, left hanging open in Bobbie's rush to get to her, CeeGee moved from her mother's side and went to the kitchen table. Again, she sat straight-backed, her feet close together, her hands clasped in front of her, just as Bobbie had found her at Mr. Tindale's.

Bobbie took a moment to call Carl at work and tell him Mr. Tindale was gone and that CeeGee had found him. "The boys are at the community pool. I need you to go pick them up," she said. "Take them somewhere and tell them what has happened, but don't bring them home until you're sure they understand. And please, call Rosa Leon. Tell her too, so she doesn't walk in on it unknowing— the way Celia Gene did." Bobbie's voice caught as she said this. "Can you do that for me?"

CeeGee could hear the warm rumbling of her father's voice through the line.

"Oh, and can you go get CeeGee's bike at Mr. Tindales's house and bring it home?" Her mother paused for his answer and then added, "Sweetie, thank you. I love you, too. Yes, I'm fine. CeeGee will be fine, too."

Bobbie hung up the phone. She sat down and reached for her daughter's hand. "Celia Gene?"

"It was cold in there," CeeGee said, staring straight ahead.

"I'm sure it was."

"His beard was grown out just a little bit. He shaved first thing every morning."

"Is that so?" Bobbie spoke quietly and gently. "That would mean he just passed in his sleep during the night. That must be the nicest way to die. Don't you think?"

"Do you think so?" CeeGee turned to look at her mother.

"I do. He had a long, wonderful life and his time had come. What could be more natural and peaceful? Like Mrs. Robins, remember?"

CeeGee's face began to crumble and her stiff mask melted away. She spoke through sobs. "I...should've ... been...there. I should have known... I should have known this was coming...and...and been there with him." She gripped her hands together so hard her knuckles turned white and she dropped her head to her chest. "He was all alone."

Bobbie spoke slowly, softly. "Celia Gene, Mr. Tindale had both of us these last weeks. He wasn't alone. I've been to see him every day for a while now."

"What?" CeeGee looked up at her. "Why did you go see my Mr. Tindale?"

Bobbie did not miss the possessive. "Just to check in on him and talk a bit. He was fine after your trip to the marsh—just a little tired, that's all. He told me all about it, he was as happy as I've ever seen him." Bobbie reached for CeeGee's hands and laid hers over them. "I've been each day since then." CeeGee's face was uncomprehending. "Here, I have a letter that he wrote to you." Bobbie rose from the table and took her purse from the counter. "It will explain everything." Bobbie pulled out a folded piece of paper, handed it to her daughter and sat back down beside her.

As CeeGee took the letter, she recognized that it was written on the same yellow legal pad they had used to make up her Guide for Giving. She could see them there, at the kitchen table, the fan blowing their hair. She pushed back her tears, unfolded the paper carefully, and began to read.

Dear Celia Gene,

If you are reading this letter, your Knowing has finally come true. Remember, I told you it would—just not on your schedule? I don't want you to be sad, child. It was my time, like it was Kenny Keller's time. Thanks to you, I didn't pass on too soon like I was aiming to, but lived my life full, right up to the natural end.

You and I never talked about this, but I want you to know that Maggie May and I couldn't have children of our own. It always left a big hole in my soul, but you filled that hole up with your loving spirit and the adventures we shared. Every day, after you and I had a visit, I passed on all the news to my dear Maggie, so maybe you filled up the hole in her soul too, if that's possible.

I knew from talking to Maggie May that I had no right to have so much of you. I thought about how your parents must be missing you, and how, if I had a little girl with a gift like yours, I'd want to share every minute of the magic and struggle of her growing up. But I liked being your friend and teacher, and so I didn't press too hard. I feel bad about that. Because I was being a selfish old man.

Then, a while back, your mother called me. She said she wanted to thank me for helping you through all

that happened with the Robins family. She said Rosa
Leon had come to see her when Mrs. Robins passed,
and your mother thought it was time she and I had a
talk. I know I told you I would stay out of it, but I went
ahead and told your mother all that had happened
with you, how you were learning, and how I thought
you needed your family back in your life. When you
accidentally told your family your Knowing about
Alice and Buster, we both knew that even if you didn't
mean to, you were sending a message to your parents,
opening the window on your gift so they might join
you and share these experiences with you—so they
might guide you.

She told me they'd been waiting for you all along and
that they were the ones who sent you to me. Now, that
one's a shocker, ain't it? It's true! Your mother sent
you over to work on my garden on purpose, thinking
I could help you understand your gift. She and your
dad figured if they couldn't be the ones to help you, I
was the next best thing. The two of them trusting me
to take care of you for a time is the greatest honor of
my long life.

So, now you are home again, and if you are reading this
letter, you need to know your mother is ready to be by
your side as you grow into the fine young woman you
are aiming to be. She can recite each one of our guidelines by heart and knows just what they mean, too.

So, don't you be sad, or blame yourself if you're not
here with me at the end. Fact is, dying is something

a body has to do alone, and I'm ready to do it. I want you to know that next to Maggie May, you've been the shining light of my life. If it's possible for me to find a way to pay you a visit and say a proper Texas goodbye, I promise to do so.

Your friend,
Samuel H. Tindale

CeeGee swiped at her chin the whole time she was reading so her tears wouldn't drip down and ruin Mr. Tindale's letter. Finally, Bobbie got up and handed her a paper towel, and CeeGee held it over her face. After she read the letter three times, she looked at her mother and said, "I don't understand. You and Dad sent me to him?"

"Yes, baby, we did. I wish your father and I could have done a better job at understanding your gift all those years ago, but we couldn't seem to find our way. We just messed things up and made it worse until finally, you shut us out. Then, no matter how hard we tried, we couldn't reach you. We knew we couldn't leave you to grapple with such a big part of yourself all alone. You needed an adult to guide you, someone who would understand and truly care for you."

"Why Mr. Tindale?"

"Next to your dad, Mr. Tindale was the best person I knew, and he always had a special way with people, especially children. I'm not like you, CeeGee. I don't have your gift, but I was able to see that Mr. Tindale had something similar. He was wise—connected to a world greater than my own. Your dad and I thought if we couldn't help you ourselves, Mr. Tindale's friendship was the best gift we could give you."

"But, Momma, all this time?"

CeeGee saw the guilt flash across her mother's face. "It was the hardest thing I've ever had to do, darlin.' Every day it was hard. But don't you think I was ever off the job." Bobbie reached across the table and put both her hands over CeeGee's clenched fists. "Celia Gene, listen to me. I know you. I carried you inside my body and I'm connected to you in a way that no one else will ever be, not even your dad, not even Mr. Tindale. Even though Mr. Tindale was your guide, I could tell what was going on. I knew when you struggled with your gift and when you were learning. I knew when you were having some fun and when things got hard. And even though it hurts me to say it, I knew Mr. Tindale was doing a better job of helping you than your father and I could. So, until Mrs. Robins passed, we stayed out of the way. Then, after she died, and I called him, Mr. Tindale and I started to talk. He was kind enough to help me like he helped you. When you told us about Alice and Buster at dinner that night, he and I both knew you were worn out from keeping your secret and needed your family, but we wanted you to have time to do it your own way, so we waited."

CeeGee looked at her mother long and hard, replaying the recent weeks in her mind, going back through all the years of hiding her gift from herself and from her parents. "May I have a drink of water, please?" she asked, unclenching her hands and stretching out her back.

Bobbie filled a glass and handed it to her, then sat in the chair next to her and pulled it up close. CeeGee drank eagerly, parched and dry from crying. She put her empty glass on the table and said, "Tell me about your visits with him, Momma."

"He told me all about your time together," Bobbie began, "what you both learned and what you meant to him. You saved his life, CeeGee, truly you did."

"I feel like he told you our private business." CeeGee lifted her chin, "Did he?"

"He never betrayed your friendship, darlin'. He was just trying to teach me before he died. He wanted to make sure I could carry on with you."

"And can you now?"

"Yes, I believe I can. When you told us about Ronnie Sampson and how you thought he could finish high school, I understood right away you needed help to give a Knowing. And I was so glad I was able to help you with that. I felt like I had made it halfway back to you." Bobbie stopped and reached back into her purse. "Here, look here," she pulled out another sheet from the same pad. She unfolded it and passed it to her daughter. There in Bobbie's neat handwriting was CeeGee's Guide for Giving. "I've memorized them," her mother said with pride, "all five of them."

CeeGee read the list and took a long look at her mother's face. Then she took another long look at Mr. Tindale's letter. At last, CeeGee reached out for her mother and Bobbie took her in her arms. They held each other in a long silence. Finally, CeeGee whispered into the familiar smell of her mother's hair, "I've missed you, Momma. I didn't even know before, but I have missed you so much."

Bobbie pulled away and cupped her daughter's cheeks in her hands. "Oh, darlin', you can't ever know how much I missed you and how glad I am to have you back." Then she reached out and tickled CeeGee, the way she did when she was little. "Now, I'm going to cook us up a big breakfast while you tell me all about all the things I've missed." She squeezed her daughter's shoulder as she rose from her chair.

CeeGee talked the whole time her mother scrambled eggs and fried up bacon and cut up leftover baked potatoes to make hash browns. Outside the window, the gray sky gathered into dense, black clouds that rolled toward the island like huge, dirty snowballs. Bobbie turned on the kitchen light. "Big storm coming in," she said as she set their plates on the table. "End of summer, it's that time of year."

The day stretched on as mother and daughter talked and talked and the blank spaces between them began to fill. When they were finally spent, it was afternoon and they were both used up. Bobbie walked her daughter to her bedroom and turned back the covers.

CeeGee took off her shoes and climbed into bed, but she had one last question, "What about Daddy?"

Bobbie sat on the edge of the bed. "I've told him all I can, darlin', but he needs to talk to you—the way we've talked. Mr. Tindale said he had a hole in his heart because he had no children. Well, your daddy has a hole in his heart from missing you. He blames himself."

"Oh, Momma, it was never his fault."

"It will mean the world to him to hear you say that." Bobbie bent over and kissed her on the forehead.

"When he gets home, I'll talk to him then."

Bobbie settled herself in the chair beside the bed, and CeeGee fell quickly to sleep.

Chapter Eighteen

At first CeeGee thought it was a close clap of thunder that awakened her, but the moment she sat up in bed the Knowing became clear and her heart began to pound. She saw her mother asleep in the chair, got up and moved quietly past her, went down the darkened stairs and into the kitchen where she saw the note from her father.

Bobbie,

Thought you girls needed your sleep.

Boys are over at the Connelly's.

Bike is in the garage.

Gone to check on the store.

I love you, both of you.
Carl

CeeGee slammed out the back door, grabbed her bike at the bottom of the steps and rode, shoeless, into the cold, wet night. The wind pushed her sideways and the lightning that lit up the sky every few seconds was followed quickly—too quickly—by a sharp crack of thunder as the full force of the storm moved over Southport. CeeGee rode as fast as she could, skidding through puddles, ignoring the rain that cut at her face and the bicycle pedals that dug into her bare feet. She did not think of where she was, only where she needed to be.

As she neared the Triple S, she could see her father's car at the curb. Inside, only the nighttime security lights were on. He must be in his office. She threw the bike down on the slick sidewalk, ran to the entry door and squeezed the latch. Open.

She pushed through the door and stepped inside. As her eyes adjusted to the dim light, she could see her father leaving his office and moving toward the pharmacy at the back of the store. Just then, CeeGee saw the jerking beam of a flashlight flit across the pharmacy wall and she heard the odd noise—a soft clatter of plastic pill bottles being swept off a shelf.

"Daddy, duck!" CeeGee yelled and started to run toward him. Carl turned around and saw her. Never taking his eyes off her, he stepped to the end of a sales counter and crouched, then held up his hands and signaled for her to stop, to get down. CeeGee tried to stop, but just then her wet, bare feet slipped on the floor and she began to slide toward her father like an ice skater gone out of control.

Carl rose and leapt out toward her like an enormous angel in flight just as CeeGee slammed into a sales rack. She felt a sharp, hot pain in her shoulder, then heard the shot and saw her father jerk slightly and thought—please, please, please—no, not him. Her knees gave way and she felt her father's strong arms wrap around her, pulling her behind the counter, away from the danger at the back of the store. They listened to the desperate, garbled words coming from the pharmacy, heard a frenzy of footsteps and a loud clang as the metal door to the alley slammed against the wall. Then, finally, silence.

"They're gone," Carl whispered. He turned to face CeeGee and helped her sit up. "Let me look at you. You've been hurt."

"Daddy, Daddy, did they shoot you?"

"I'm fine, hush. I'm fine…"

"But they, the gun…"

CeeGee and her father talked over each other as they searched for wounds, peering in the dim light, looking for signs of blood. Carl pushed up the sleeve on CeeGee's shirt and stroked the bruise on her shoulder. It was already purple and angry. CeeGee discovered a tear in the sleeve of her father's shirt and they both looked in surprise at a tiny river of bright, red blood trickling down his arm and dripping off his elbow. She pulled back the bloody fabric and saw a narrow, shallow groove carved into the flesh of his arm.

"Oh, Daddy, they did, they shot you. It's my fault… I knew… I should have…"

"Don't you dare say that," Carl ordered and put his fingers to her lips. "I will not have you blame yourself for what you know, or what you don't know, ever again. If there is blame, it is mine."

"But, Daddy…"

"It is not your job to take care of me. It is mine—*my job*—to take care of *you*."

"But I…"

"Here look," he held out his arm. "It's barely a nick, it's nothing. Now hush, just let me hold you." He wrapped his arms around her and pulled her against his chest, as if he needed to shield her even now.

CeeGee, trembling from cold and fear and relief, gave up talking and curled into his embrace, sniffing at him like a blind puppy. "Daddy. My Daddy."

Carl held her silently until she stopped trembling, then helped her to her feet.

"I have to put a bandage on your arm," she said.

"It's fine. It can wait."

"No, it has to have a bandage, and antiseptic," CeeGee insisted.

"All right. You go get the stuff. I'll call the police."

CeeGee went to the first aid section of the store and found tape, a box of cotton balls, a roll of gauze and a bottle of hydrogen peroxide. She carried it all back to his office, sat on the chair in front of his desk and listened to his strong, calm voice over the phone as he reported the robbery and shooting to the police. Then he pulled his desk chair around close to hers and sat down next to her.

They talked of little things while she looked at the spot where the bullet grazed his arm, then cleaned and bandaged the wound, but when she heard the high-pitched wail of the sirens, her back went stiff and she reached out for her father. They were coming again, the men in uniforms with all their noise, confusion and tragedy. For the second time in a day.

Carl took CeeGee's elbow and helped her up. They stepped out into the store as Southport's entire police force and emergency medical team began swarming toward them like ants over a carcass. CeeGee moved closer to her father.

"Carl, what happened here? You two all right?" a policeman said as he rushed toward them.

"Hey, Frank. Yes, we are," Carl said, "but my daughter's shaken. I need to take her outside for a minute, give her a chance to calm down. I'll come right back and tell you all about what happened."

He pointed to the back of the store, to the pharmacy section. "They took some meds off the shelves and left through the back of the store, you can check there."

As they moved to the front door, a medic rushed toward them with a bag in his hand. "Hey, wait up!" he shouted. "We heard there were injuries."

CeeGee turned her face into her father's chest, "Daddy, please," she whispered.

"We're all right, really. Just give us a minute, Joe." Carl moved CeeGee to the side where there was no bandage, and CeeGee clutched her father's arm as they moved to the door. He touched her back as he guided her through. They walked into the clean air and crossed the street. The storm had passed, and the night was quiet, dark and still, the pavement cool and wet on CeeGee's bare feet. Carl brushed the drops of water from a sidewalk bench, and CeeGee and her father sat down next to each other and looked back toward the store. Five white police cars and two yellow emergency vans were parked in front and two policemen moved along the wet sidewalk, the light from their flashlights crisscrossing back and forth.

Carl began to talk about thunderstorms, pulling CeeGee's thoughts away from the scene in front of them. "You know how Texans have to brag about everything?" he said. "They say they have the biggest thunderstorms on earth, like it doesn't happen anywhere else the way it does here. They make it sound like a Greek drama, with the gods throwing spears of lightning from the heavens and beating gigantic drums of thunder. The rain comes down as if poured from colossal buckets. If you weren't from Texas and didn't know better, you'd think it was the end of the world."

He paused a moment and CeeGee said, "Keep on going, Daddy."

"These native Texans boast that they can sleep straight through the din of a storm like we had tonight. No more to them than a train passing by."

As she listened to her father's words, CeeGee looked up at the black night sky. She felt her heart slow down. She shook out her neck and shoulders like a dog shaking off water. She thought about Mr. Tindale and wondered if he had brought the storm, and the

Knowing, to say a big Texas goodbye to her, the way he promised in his letter.

Just then, Danny and Davey rode around the corner on their bikes, flung them on the sidewalk and ran inside the Triple S. Seconds later, Bobbie's car screeched to a stop at the end of the line of police cars. She threw open her door and ran for the entrance too.

"I'll go get them," Carl said. "You stay right here. I'll bring them back to you." He gave her knee a pat as he rose, then loped across the street, calling out to his wife. Bobbie turned at the sound of his voice. When he reached her, they put their arms around each other and he bent down to whisper in her ear. Bobbie pulled back, looked at his torn and bloodied shirtsleeve and touched the bandage gently.

A policeman came to the doorway of the store and pointed at Carl and Bobbie. The twins pushed past him and ran to their parents. Carl pulled both boys close and kissed them on the tops of their heads. He pointed to CeeGee sitting on her bench waiting for them. The family turned and began to walk toward her. Carl had his arm around his wife's waist and Bobbie was leaning in to him. The boys were on each side, almost as tall as Bobbie now. The halo of the streetlight lit all of them from above and the wet pavement sparkled under their feet like diamonds.

CeeGee stood up and stepped off the curb toward them. Just then, they all heard a loud whooshing sound. The family looked up and saw a bright, white light as it ripped across the sky, sliced the heavens in two and disappeared into the vast, black beyond. CeeGee lifted her face to the light as if it held warmth and comfort for the few seconds before it was gone.

The twins jumped back. "What the...! Dad, was that a shooting star?"

Carl gazed up at the sky and shook his head. "That was no shooting star. That was like nothing I've ever seen."

"Celia Gene?" Bobbie asked.

CeeGee pulled her gaze back to her mother and took in her family, the four of them standing together, waiting for her. She took the last two steps toward them.

"Why, don't y'all know?" she said, grinning and proud. "That was my Mr. Tindale—passing on through."

Chapter Nineteen

The day of Mr. Tindale's funeral dawned clear and cool. CeeGee thought that maybe he ordered it up that way since he'd been planning exactly how he wanted it for months. If he could streak across the sky like a comet to say goodbye to her, she figured he could make it a nice day for his own funeral.

CeeGee looked at herself in the mirror and turned around to see her new purple satin dress from all angles. She couldn't remember the last time she wore a dress and thought it actually made her look like a girl, instead of a skinny, shapeless stick that could be anything. It was the color of grape juice, with a high neck, an empire waist and a skirt that belled out at the bottom.

Bobbie stuck her head in CeeGee's room. "Time to go, darlin'. We need to get there a little early." She turned to walk away, then turned back. "You look beautiful, by the way."

"You too, Momma." Bobbie's shining crimson hair was piled up on top of her head with little curls escaping in the back. She had on a fitted black dress with long sleeves that hugged her curves and made her skin look the palest pink.

A few days after Mr. Tindale died, Bobbie got a phone call from a lawyer, Mr. Antonio. He said that he was representing Mr. Tindale's estate, and told Bobbie that it was Mr. Tindale's wish that Bobbie deliver a eulogy at his funeral as his friend in the community. CeeGee had to go look up the word *eulogy* and found that it meant *tribute* or *acclamation*. She looked up those words too and came to understand that a eulogy was a speech to honor and praise someone after their death.

Mr. Antonio said that Mr. Tindale cherished his friendship with Celia Gene, but he didn't ask her to give his eulogy because he thought she would feel too shy in front of such a big group, especially at a time like this. Bobbie told Mr. Antonio that she would be honored to give the eulogy and would work with CeeGee on what to say.

Mr. Antonio also said that Mr. Tindale's brother, Earl from Indiana, would be coming to the island to deliver a second eulogy on behalf of the Tindale family. CeeGee was amazed that she did not even know there was an Earl from Indiana and began to wonder what else she didn't know about her own best friend. She kept trying to feel Mr. Tindale around her, the way he felt Maggie May after she passed. She wanted to ask him about his brother, but her friend wasn't there.

A lot of people were already there, even though it was early. The Williamsons sat down in their reserved seats in the front row, and Bobbie pulled her notes out of her purse to read them over. Danny and Davey started to complain that their new suits were too itchy, and Carl shushed them before they even finished the sentence. CeeGee turned around in her seat to watch the pavilion as it filled up. If someone wanted to rob a house, she decided, this day would be just as good as the Fourth of July, because nobody in the entire town of Southport would be at home. There was a line of people down the aisle and onto the grass outside waiting to get seats. The police were directing cars to park in the ferry overflow lot.

Mr. Tindale had arranged in advance for Sandwith Brothers' Funeral Home to set up the big open-air pavilion next to the ferry landing with chairs and flowers and a podium at the front next to his beautiful casket, which was open, of course. It was a hot August morning, but the roofed pavilion offered shade, and a slight breeze was coming off the channel and wafted softly through the open space. Behind the casket, set up high on an easel, was the painting of the marsh by Mrs. Tindale.

Mike Robins was in the third row, Rosa Leon was next to him and then Juan with one Robins kid on his lap and three more between him and Rosa. Then the line of people at the back all moved aside, and CeeGee saw they were making room for Ronnie Sampson to get past in his wheelchair. One of the ushers from Sandwith Brothers pulled a folding chair from an aisle and motioned for Ronnie to roll his wheelchair into the open spot. CeeGee smiled, turned back around and stood up so she could see Mr. Tindale lying so peacefully in his casket, the blue pinstripes of his burial suit matching perfectly with the blue satin lining they had put in the casket. She knew the real Mr. Tindale was gone from his body, but it was good to see him again anyway, for this one last time.

Finally, Earl from Indiana, who looked just like his brother, only taller and skinnier, rose and walked to the podium. He began to speak about his brother as a boy and a young man. He told how Mr. and Mrs. Tindale met all the way back in high school and, for the first time, the people of Southport learned how Mr. Tindale's leg got injured. He was in the war and a grenade went off amid a group of soldiers. Even though he was hurt, he kept going back into the smoke and fire trying to save his fellow soldiers. When Earl told them all that his brother was awarded a Silver Star for this act of bravery, the whole place started applauding. CeeGee didn't think it was proper to applaud at a funeral and wondered where Miss McGuire was sitting and what she thought of that.

Next Bobbie rose from her seat, set her notes on the chair and went to the podium. She stood quietly for a moment and looked over the crowd, then she began to talk about Mr. Tindale. She said Mr. Tindale spent his whole life being kind and generous, especially to children. He had a way of listening to young folks that let them know he understood and cared for them. Even though he and his beloved wife, Maggie May, never had children of their own, they set an example for every parent and teacher in Southport to follow. Then she listed the rules he lived by, which CeeGee wrote down on her program so she wouldn't ever forget, even though she already had them memorized in her guide.

1. Give Your Gifts.
2. Follow the Golden Rule.
3. Do not Judge.
4. Look for silver linings—because things that seem bad at first may turn out good in the end.
5. If you can change your direction, you can change your whole future.

CeeGee was crying by the time Bobbie finished and hoped that wherever he was, Mr. Tindale was listening to this for himself. She imagined him like a soft light, hovering above them, looking down on this beautiful scene. He'd be pleased that it all turned out so perfectly, and a little embarrassed to have so much public praise.

☆☆☆☆

A week later, Mr. Antonio called again. This time he asked CeeGee and her parents to come to his office for the reading of Mr. Tindale's will. When they arrived, he had chairs set up for the three of them, plus Earl from Indiana, the principal of the high school and—what a surprise—Miss Frances McGuire.

Once they settled in, Mr. Antonio sat down behind his big mahogany desk and began to read. First, he told them that Mr. Tindale's house and all the contents would be sold and the proceeds added to the estate. Mr. Antonio explained that this was because

Mr. Tindale wanted to take all the money in his estate and use it to help children on the island. He planned to set up a fund that would, first, pay for Celia Gene Williamson's college education. Then the fund would continue to provide scholarships for other Southport children.

On top of that, Mr. Tindale would give enough money to the Southport Public Library for Miss McGuire to finish building her children's storytelling room and study room for teens exactly the way she wanted, with extra to add the meeting room and buy all the books she needed to fill up the bookcases for years to come. CeeGee thought Miss McGuire must have really done some talking when she took her Books and Brownies to Mr. T.'s house.

Then Mr. Antonio passed around copies of the American Library Association's Recommended List of books for children and teens. He told Miss McGuire the ALA lists would be her guide for book purchases for young people. Miss McGuire started to sputter about how she knew perfectly well what books to buy for her own public library and how it was her job to protect island youth from nefarious literature, but it didn't do any good. Mr. Antonio just smiled at her and said, "You are perfectly free to use other funds to buy the books of your choosing. These funds from Samuel Tindale will be used to buy the books on the American Library Association's annual lists."

Miss McGuire squirmed and harrumphed but didn't say anything more. Carl and Bobbie covered their faces with their hands to keep from laughing out loud.

Finally, Mr. Antonio told Earl and CeeGee they had permission to take anything they wanted from the house before it was sold. CeeGee looked over at Earl to see if he was upset that he didn't get any money. Like he could read her mind, he turned to her and said, "Child, I have everything I need in life." He sounded just like Mr. Tindale.

✩ ✩ ✩ ✩

CeeGee couldn't bring herself to go to Mr. Tindale's house for weeks. She waited so long the police had time to solve the robbery at the Triple S. It was the first armed robbery on Magdalena Island in twenty-seven years and the police were so excited about having an actual crime to solve they dragged it out for as long as they possibly could, strutting around town and interviewing people and taking fingerprints.

Truth was, it was so easy CeeGee could have solved it herself. The police figured out from the rubber tire marks in the alley that the robbers came and left through the rear delivery door to the stock room. They also saw there wasn't any damage to the door or the lock. They brought in the stock room boy and after they talked to him a while, he admitted he got money for leaving the door unlocked but said he didn't steal anything. After they talked to him a while longer, he told them who gave him the money—three guys from Ronnie Sampson's old gang.

The police rounded them up and they confessed their plan was to get into the pharmacy and steal some medicine that they could sell. They said Carl Williamson surprised them when he came to check on the store and they accidentally shot him. This didn't help them at all, because when they went to trial, the judge said it was no *accident* they brought a gun with them in the first place. All three were convicted. The stock boy got a year of probation and community service, two of the robbers were sent to detention until their twenty-first birthdays and the shooter went to prison for three years.

It was too bad for them, but the whole thing really lit a fire under Ronnie Sampson. He had already been studying for his high school graduation requirements, but after his old buddies got arrested, he started working even harder. Having a goal in life was making Ronnie handsomer by the day. Now, each school day he wheeled himself the four blocks to the high school and after he finished his studies, he went over to the gym where the coach was teaching him how to lift weights to make his body stronger. He got his hair cut nice and neat and the twins said that girls at the high school were flirting with him.

CeeGee's Knowing was starting to come true. Bobbie thought Ronnie had a good chance of getting a scholarship to art school, but she wasn't going to butt in. She said she would follow the rules by allowing Ronnie the time to change his own direction and make his own bright new future.

The twins started begging for the stock boy's job at the Triple S, because they were going to be sixteen soon and needed to save up money for the car their parents were never going to buy them. Carl said they should go out and interview and find their own job, not get one so easy from him. But they begged and argued, and finally Bobbie chimed in, too.

She said that maybe it was time for Carl to get to know his sons, find out who they really were. She said they wanted a job and they wanted to buy their own car, why couldn't he be proud of them? Then the twins reminded their dad that if they'd been the ones working in the stock room, there never would have been any robbery at all. Carl had to allow that all this was true, so he quit being stubborn and hired them.

In no time, they started complaining that work got in the way of going to the beach with their friends and, besides that, it put them in the same category as Johnny Johanssen, which they thought was 'mortifying'. CeeGee thought that was a good word but knew it would never work with her parents. Naturally, Carl and Bobbie wouldn't let them quit. They said the new job kept the boys out of trouble, plus it gave them a valuable opportunity to learn a lesson in humility.

Once they gave up whining, Danny and Davey started to do well at the store. Danny conducted a survey with all the high school girls on the island to find out what brands of makeup they liked and where they bought it. He made up a chart with the results and showed it to his dad. As a result, Carl ordered four new kinds of makeup and soon a lot more of the island's high school girls were shopping in the cosmetic aisle at the Triple S instead of going to the mainland. Davey made up his own chart for storing stuff in the stock room. He put the things that needed to be replaced most often on the lowest shelves and the things that were slower to sell up on the top shelves. Carl began to view his sons differently and started to listen to what they had to say, instead of butting in all the time and treating them like two disasters waiting to happen.

Every time Bobbie saw the three of them talking together, she got all teary-eyed and gave CeeGee a big hug. CeeGee figured Bobbie hugged her because the twins wouldn't let their mother hug them. They thought it was sissy.

☆☆☆☆

Finally, Mr. Antonio called and said he had a buyer for Mr. Tindale's house. If CeeGee wanted anything from it, now was the time to make her choices. The next day, CeeGee worked up the courage to go. It was a warm day and as she walked over she thought and thought about what she should take that would help her remember her good friend. She let herself into the living room. The light slanted through the half-open blinds and little dust motes danced in the air. CeeGee stood in the middle of the room for a while, hoping Mr. Tindale would tell her what to do, but nothing came. She guessed he'd already said goodbye and was leaving it up to her to figure things out.

She went back out to the front porch, got his old rocker and put it at the bottom of the stairs. Then she went to the garage workshop and found the bucket filled with Mrs. Tindale's garden tools and put that on the seat of the rocker. She went to the kitchen and took the pocket knife that he used to peel their apples out of the drawer and put it in her back pocket. Finally, she went over to the bookcase in the living room to see if she could find Mr. T's old copy of John Steinbeck's *Cannery Row* on one of the shelves. She remembered sitting at the kitchen table with Mr. Tindale and how he looked through the book for the story of the Great Tide Pool that helped them understand her gift. He told her Steinbeck showed how the tide pool was a just a tiny world, but beyond it a greater world existed, and had its influence. He said, like a creature in a tide pool, CeeGee was just a small piece of something so big she couldn't be expected to understand the vastness of it all.

Then CeeGee saw a small package propped up on the living room shelf, right at eye level. It was wrapped in brown paper, like a paper bag from a grocery store, with a string of twine tied up in a bow. On the front of the package was written, *CeeGee's Gift*. CeeGee recognized Mr. Tindale's handwriting and tried not to cry. She took the package from the shelf, sat down on the chair and opened it. It was just what she hoped to find, but even more. Tucked inside the cover was a sheet from the big yellow pad, his own handwritten list of CeeGee's Guide for Giving, only his didn't have 'Never Tell the Parents Anything' at the end. Plus, there was a photograph of Mr. Tindale sitting on the front porch in his rocker and petting Spunk the Cat. He was grinning at the camera big as life. CeeGee knew immediately that her mother had taken that picture after she and Mr. Tindale became friends. CeeGee fought back tears as she looked at his dear face. She turned the photograph over. He had written on the back, 'For Celia Gene. From your good friend forever, Samuel Tindale.'

She stood up, held up the picture and pretended he was looking at her instead of the camera. "Mr. Tindale," she said out loud, "I will always save this picture. It comforts me that you took such care to let me know you are my friend. Since I can't tell you in person, I'm going to trust that you know how much I appreciate our friendship and all you taught me."

She dropped her hand to her side, thought a minute, then lifted the picture up again. "I will work to be the person you believe I can be. I will make good grades, I will get into a good college and make myself worthy of my gift from you. I promise to give my Knowings with kindness and generosity, and look for silver linings, and all the other important things you taught me."

Chapter Twenty

Dear Mr. Tindale,

Hello from earth. It's been a year since you passed on and I've been thinking and thinking about you. I really miss you and need to talk to you, but just brooding about it isn't making me feel any better, so I decided to write you a letter. I put your picture in a nice big frame, and I'm going to put my letter to you where you left one for me, inside the cover of *Cannery Row,* and trust that somehow it will reach you. Even if it doesn't, I figure writing to you will make me feel better.

I haven't had a Knowing since you left this earth, not for this whole year. I keep waiting and anticipating, but nothing. I'm trying to figure out why. I wonder if it's because you aren't here to guide and teach me anymore. Maybe having Knowings wasn't just my gift, but yours and mine together. Now that you're gone, they're gone.

I talked to my mother about it and she was some help. I can hear you right now saying, 'See, I told you so. You should talk to your mother about these important things.' She said I shouldn't worry, that if a Knowing is needed, one will come. She said I'm not being 'called to serve' at this time. I thought that was a nice expression, 'called to serve.'

Elby said because of all I have learned from the Knowings and from you, I can understand people's needs and struggles in a way other people can't so easily, so maybe I don't need the Knowings. I can just be observant and try to help people any way I can. Elby says I am a 'sympathetic soul'. I remember your halo of light and how we thought it helped you understand the needs and feelings of others. Maybe now I have a little halo like you did, which would be an honor, like I can take your place and follow in your halo instead of your footsteps. I'd prefer to talk to you about this in person, but I'll have to admit my mom and Elby have been a comfort. If you have any other advice, please let me know—somehow.

As long as I'm writing, I should fill you in on all the news around here. First off, guess who bought your house? Mike Robins! Mike told me that Mr. Antonio offered him a special deal, so he could afford to buy the house even though he was still building his business and didn't have too much money saved yet. I have a feeling you might have had something to do with that deal.

Juan and Rosa are still working for Mike, so Maggie May's garden looks great and everything in your house is spic and span, just the way you like it. Now that there are four little kids running around, Rosa has her hands full keeping things up to your standards. I keep telling her that you would rather have the Robins kids living in your house than have it neat as a pin, but you know Rosa.

Mike told me he always thought you had the best garage workshop in town, and he said that even after he bought his big-ass fan, excuse my language, his carport was still a poor excuse for a workshop. Your garage was already empty because your brother Earl from Indiana took your old car to remember you by. Earl said when he left Southport he was going to tour the whole USA in that big, ugly boat of yours.

You should see the garage workshop now. Mike has those same pegboards on the wall with an outline for every tool, just like before. The place smells like fresh wood, and it's filled up with all the caskets Mike is making now that he's finished the library! After working with Miss McGuire, Mike got new business cards made that said, 'Custom Cabinets' as well as 'Custom Caskets'. He passed them around town and told people, "If I can do work for Frances McGuire, I can do work for anybody."

So, thanks to you, the Southport Public Library now has a storytelling room for children and a study room for teens. Actually, they aren't rooms, but spaces set apart by the big, new bookcase dividers Mike made, so they seem cozy and private. The teen study area has six great big tables, so we have room to spread out all our books and papers. All the teenagers in town go to the library to do their homework, which is nice, especially for the kids who don't have a space at home.

Miss McGuire painted the children's storytelling room blue and white to make it look like the sky. Mike Robins made kid-sized tables and refinished the little chairs he found second hand. There is a big cloud painted on the floor where the children sit when a volunteer reads them a story. They look like a bunch of little cherubs sitting on that cloud. The best part of the room is a glass display case sitting up on wooden legs that Mike also made.

Guess why? So, Miss McGuire could put Ronnie Sampson's entire collection of bird carvings in it! Ronnie showed her his birds when she delivered 'Books and Brownies' like I hoped he would, and after she got the money from you she bought the whole collection. Ronnie is saving every cent she paid him, hoping he can use the money for college someday, and we know he will.

The little kids crowd around Ronnie's birds like they are at a zoo. First thing every morning, Miss McGuire gets out her spray bottle and cleans all the little kid-sized handprints off the glass from the day before. She put up a sign on the wall next to the birds that says _Do Not Touch the Glass_, but it doesn't do any good. I nearly bust out crying every time I see those birds. They look like they are living right where they belong—sitting all together like a little flock. I can almost hear them chirping.

Oh, and one last thing, Miss McGuire filled all the new shelves with books from the American Library Association's recommended list like you instructed in your will. Now that she's read all the books herself, she actually admits it was a pretty good rule you made. Can you believe it? Expanding the library and taking people Books and Brownies has truly made Miss McGuire a nicer person. She doesn't boss people around every second the way she used to, and she smiles more. Now, instead of dreaming about her fake Knight in Shining Armor, she has a chance to find her real true love like in my Knowing.

I have learned from her, and from you, that if I want to feel better on the inside, I just need to get outside myself and go do something nice for other people. In accordance with this, Elby and I volunteered to put the new library books on the shelves, but in spite of our good intentions, we got in trouble a few times because Miss McGuire kept catching us reading instead of shelving.

Now I have some not so good news. Alice Adams, now Alice McCall, did have a baby like in my Knowing, and they are struggling to take care of him. They live in a little one-room apartment on top of someone's garage and barely have enough to take care of themselves, much less a baby. Buster works at the gas station fixing cars, but he doesn't make much money. My dad says that's because he isn't very good at it.

I thought it might help if I babysat for them one night a week, so they could get out alone together for a date night and maybe stay in love. My dad said that would be okay, but only if he dropped me off and picked me up. He says that it is his job to keep me safe, even though I am fourteen now.

I just read this letter over and the last part doesn't seem too cheerful. I don't know if you ever get down in the dumps where you are, but just in case, I'll end with a funny story. Toward the end of the library project, Mike Robins was working day and night, trying to keep up with his caskets and get finished with the library before school let out and the place filled up with kids and tourists. Miss McGuire decided to help him out by taking care of his kids after Rosa went home in the evening, which thrilled him to no end, as you can imagine.

Here's the funny part. After she put the children to bed, Miss McGuire went to work organizing Mike's house. I know you can picture all the cupboards and closets since it used to be your house. She dug into each and every one, folded all the towels in thirds and stacked them perfectly, grouped the cleaning products according to her own special categories, rearranged the pots, pans and dishes and even moved things from one cupboard to another. She pestered Mike to make her a spice rack to hang on the kitchen wall, so she could put all his seasonings on the rack in alphabetical order.

Mike says Miss McGuire has her own personal Dewey Decimal System for houses, but he doesn't understand it and neither does Rosa. Rosa can't find her cleaning supplies and Mike can't find the griddle or the egg poaching pan. Every day, Mike has to ask Miss McGuire where she put stuff. Can't you just see Miss McGuire bustling around the house, cluck-clucking, folding and arranging? I love it that she alphabetized the spices.

Well, I guess that's all the news for now. I feel better for having written to you, just like I hoped I would. If I get a Knowing, I'll let you know right away.

Love and hugs from your best friend forever,
Celia Gene Williamson

P.S. Juan and Rosa adopted Spunk, so don't worry, he has a happy home.

Chapter Twenty-One

Dear Mr. Tindale,

I've been thinking about you all the time lately. A lot has happened since I wrote you two years ago, and it all makes me miss you and want to talk to you. I will catch you up on everything, but first I must tell you about tonight. I just got home from my brothers' graduation from Southport High School. Guess who graduated along with Danny and Davey? Ronnie Sampson! It reminded me of your funeral because the whole town was there. Everyone knows how hard Ronnie had to work to earn his high school diploma and they all came to cheer him on. This makes me so proud of Southport. People around here used to blame Ronnie for every bad thing that happened, but when he changed and tried to make his life better, our whole town changed right along with him. My dad, and the other men from the Town Club who made the wheelchair ramp at Ronnie's house, went over to the football field and made a ramp up to the stage so he could get his own diploma. He's so strong from working out with the high school coach that he wheeled himself up that steep ramp like it was nothing.

After the principal handed Ronnie his diploma and shook his hand, he made him stay on the stage while he went to the microphone and announced that Ronnie had received a full scholarship to an art school right in the middle of movie-making land in California—just like Elby figured from my Knowing. Elby, who was sitting next to me, punched me in the ribs to remind me. The entire audience gave Ronnie a standing ovation. Can you imagine? His mother was sitting a few seats down from us and I leaned over to see what she'd do. She looked around at all the people cheering for her son like it didn't make any sense to her, then she started to cry and never stopped until the principal handed out the last diploma.

I'm glad Ronnie gets to go away to school in California where people will only know him as the fine person he is right now. No one will know about his past, so it won't get in his way or hold him back. I think that's why some people need to leave home when they grow up, so they are free to step into their future, instead of staying stuck in their past forever.

Now, on to the next news. Alice McCall is pregnant—again. My father says Buster and Alice need to come in for a conference with their pharmacist, so he can explain BIRTH CONTROL to them. (You know how he likes to say certain words real loud.) After Alice had the first baby, my mom helped her get a part-time job at the high school, and Alice's mom helped out with the baby, so Alice could earn some money. When Alice found out she was pregnant again, she went blubbering to the high school guidance counselor about how she was afraid she would just keep having babies one after another and she didn't think she could handle it. She said Buster wasn't earning enough money for them to have more children, and they were fighting all the time, and she was scared that nothing would ever be right between them.

The guidance counselor set the two of them up with a marriage counselor, and Buster was miserable enough that he agreed to go. I babysit for them twice a week now—once for the date night and once so they can go see the marriage counselor. Alice tells me all about it when they get home. They are making new decisions every week. There will be no more yelling and swearing at each other. They made up a chart to show the chores they have each agreed to do and a strict budget to help with their finances. Buster is working at the marina now and studying to become a certified marine mechanic, and he looks like he is proud of himself. My mom says that for two people who went steady for six years, they sure didn't know each other very well. My dad says they never took their hands off each other long enough to have a simple conversation. But they are talking now and willing to change the direction they were headed, which means they can change their future. Through all of this, I can see that Alice and Buster truly love each other, like they have since they were kids. That bad part of my Knowing isn't going to keep coming true and this takes a great burden off my shoulders. I know, I know, I didn't cause their problems, but you know how I am.

Alice and Buster aren't the only ones changing direction. Miss McGuire has found her real-life knight! You will never guess who it is. Here's a clue—Magdalena Island's most famous hermit. It turns out that on Books and Brownies night, Miss McGuire always went to Ernest Hughes' place last, out by the saltwater pond. Once he got used to her coming around, he started making a bonfire on the beach and they would stay up late into the night talking about books and ideas. I'm guessing Miss McGuire did the talking and Ernest did the listening, which would make them the perfect couple. Everyone knew something was up because Miss McGuire started humming all the time. My mom says humming is a sure sign that someone is truly in love. After a few months, Miss McGuire announced she and Ernest were going off the island to get married and then on to England to see where all the famous writers lived. Before they left, Ernest gave Mike Robins the money to remodel his house by the saltwater pond and make it just perfect for him and his new bride. Miss McGuire is still humming.

As for me, I haven't had a Knowing for three years. I feel like my radio has turned off and there is no signal passing by anymore. Elby and my mom say that even without the Knowings I seem to think about things that other kids my age don't thinking about yet, like why people do the things they do and how I can help make things better. Maybe that's how it will be from now on. So, I am going to keep thinking about what I would do if I did have a Knowing, and how you would advise me. It's like I used to feel so separate—a too tall, skinny girl with strange Knowings. Now I feel more like I am part of everything, so I am just paying attention to see where I can fit in and help out.

Even though I'm not so odd anymore, I'm still too tall and skinny, but the boys are starting to catch up. Not that they interest me one bit, except for Elby, who is still my best friend and is a sophomore with me at Southport High. After eighth grade, he told his parents he didn't want to go to private school on the mainland anymore. They finally realized he was going to stay smart no matter where he went to school; plus they were tired of all the driving, so they let him switch.

Elby is now good friends with Kim Soon too, which is okay with me because I like them both. The Soon family has opened another business in Southport. They leased the space next door to the Asian Pearl restaurant to start a Tae Kwon Do school. Billy Joe Jones had been studying Tae Kwon Do with Kim since they had their big fight, and now they both teach there. Billy Joe has the youngest kids in his class. My brothers take classes there and they saw Billy Joe when he was teaching. They told me he was very kind and patient with the children. Maybe he remembers how he used to feel when he was the little runt and got picked on. He is helping these kids to be kinder and stronger than he was.

As for me, I'm trying not to be such a loner. When I started high school, I decided I would try to make some new friends by sitting at the cafeteria table with those giggly girls I used to make fun of all the time. I forced myself to listen to their silliness and in time, I got over feeling like I was going to throw up. Occasionally, they even said something slightly interesting. This year, a new girl came to Southport High who reminded me of me. She was so shy she could barely open her mouth to speak. I invited her to sit at our lunch table and at first the giggly girls acted like I'd broken a rule, but I kept inviting her anyway. Little by little, they got used to her, and she got used to them, so now she fits in. In fact, she is giggling, too. My mom says I need to re-member my guide and not judge those girls. She says, "Celia Gene, giggling is not a character flaw." I know you would say the exact same thing, so I'm trying.

I am also trying to be honest and admit that all my criticizing and stubbornness is just a crusty shield I put up to hide behind. I've always been a tall, skinny book-worm, too shy to make friends, plus I felt like a freak because of my Knowings. Instead of learning how to make friends, I acted like I didn't want any. If I look at it this way, I have to admit that I've been the one acting stupid, not the giggly girls. I told my mom this one day while we were having our Dr. Peppers and eating chips and salsa after school, and she got that weepy look she gets sometimes, like I'm her newborn baby. I asked her what that look meant and she said, "You are becoming the woman I saw in you as a child." I guess that's just about the nicest thing she could ever say to me.

Speaking of weeping, there is a lot of it going on at our house. In the fall, the twins will leave for college at the University of Texas and my parents are in mourning. I am in mourning, too. I know when you were here the twins and I didn't get along that well, but once Danny and Davey started working for my dad and all of us kids were in high school, my family got closer. My brothers got their own car and my parents made them drive me everywhere, like to football games, down to the beach and for sodas at the Triple S on weekends. It has given us a chance to get to know each other better. My parents might have done that on purpose because they're smart that way, you know?

I remember when the twins went off to first grade. I missed them so much. My mother used to make me graham cracker and peanut butter sandwiches and I would go outside and sit on the upstairs porch for hours, watching down the street, waiting for them to come home from school. Come fall, I feel like I will be sitting and watching and waiting until Thanksgiving for my brothers to come home. They are only going to the University of Texas in Austin, but it feels like they are leaving earth.

Mr. Tindale, all of this news makes me think of being with you and all we did together—helping Ronnie, Mike Robins, Alice and Buster, Miss McGuire, Billy Joe and Kim, my family. Even though they all faced hard time and tragedies, loneliness and heartbreak, they got a chance to get a hold of their lives and their future, make better choices and change the direction they were headed. Now, even from afar, it feels like you are still helping me learn how to make friends. I don't think any of these lives would have turned out the way they did if you hadn't lived in Southport, helped me with my Knowings and taught me how I could use my gift in a generous way. That's what this letter is really about. I want to thank you one more time and let you know that Southport is a better place because you lived among us. I hope things are going well for you, wherever you are.

Your best friend forever,
CeeGee

Chapter Twenty-Two

Dear Mr. Tindale,

This is an important letter and I want to make sure I say things exactly right. I've been thinking about writing you for a long time and I believe I'm ready to share my thoughts and feelings with you, the way they are inside of me. Tonight, five years after your passing, I will go to my high school graduation. I will climb the stairs to the stage to receive my diploma and, just like Ronnie Sampson, the principal will ask me to stand beside him while he announces that I have received a scholarship to the college of my choice. From you.

I'm old enough now to realize what your gift means to me, my family, my future and to all the other kids you will help after me. You gave me the freedom to spend my high school years dreaming about what I wanted to be when I grew up, knowing I would have all the support I needed to become that person. Your gift has made my world so much bigger. With Miss McGuire's help, I spent my high school years reading dozens of biographies about people with many different and exciting careers: scientists and artists, historians and

architects, politicians and teachers. I spent long afternoons on my bed reading and dreaming, knowing that
if I had the talent and the will, any of those pursuits
were open to me. I wish all children could be free to
dream as I have. I don't think there is a greater gift.

Tonight when the principal makes his announce-
ment, he will say I am going to attend the University
of Washington, where my parents went to college
and where they met and fell in love. 'It may seem like
I am trying to get as far away from Southport as I
can, but that's not why I'm going to Washington.' I
still love Magdalena Island, but I am ready to leave
home and find my grown up self. My mother says
I've turned into a swan, which is her nice way of ad-
mitting that I used to be an ugly duckling, right?
Maybe she sees a swan on the outside, but on the
inside, I still feel like that strange and gangly girl who
didn't fit in very well.

I know I'm not that person anymore, and I know I
helped a lot of people with my Knowings, but it's like
that old feeling is locked inside me and can't get out as
long as I stay on this island. I am ready to go away from
here, meet new people and have them meet me. I want
to find out who I am now. The way Ronnie Sampson
did. The way Elby will do at Stanford University, where
he has his own scholarship, of course.

I'm going to need your help a little longer than four
years, because to reach my goal I need a Masters' degree.
Your attorney, Mr. Antonio, said your scholarship fund

would support my graduate school tuition because he knows you would approve of my career choice. Guess what? I've decided to become a librarian! There, aren't you excited? It's exactly what I want to do, but I thought it would please you, too. I've researched colleges that offer graduate degrees in library science. I could stay right in Washington, or go up to British Columbia, or even come back to the University of Texas with Danny and Davey.

Time will tell, but no matter where I end up, I promise to do my best to make you and my parents proud. My dad is hoping that when I finish school I will come home to Southport and take over for Miss McGuire, so she can retire, but I'm not making any promises. I want to see where life leads me. Besides, I don't think my parents are so sad to see me go, not the way they were with Danny and Davey. I can see them looking past me to their own future, on their own and still in love, the way they started out.

Since my parents found love in Seattle, maybe I will, too. I've still never had a real boyfriend, but I think I might be ready. Maybe I will find someone who wants to take walks with me on gray, drizzly days and throw crusts of bread to the seagulls wheeling in from the bay, the way my parents used to do. I'd like to sit by a fire and talk about books and ideas all night like Miss McGuire and Ernest Hughes. And be able to say just what I think, and feel safe being me, like I am with Elby. Maybe I will find someone who would linger for a while, even after death, to share old memories like

Maggie May did with you. It seems an impossible vision, but I tell myself that even though my dad was a shy, awkward boy, a special person like my mother fell in love with him. This gives me hope.

Enough about me. There is news from Southport. Last summer, Ronnie Sampson came home from California for a visit. I went by to see him and he looked even better than when he left, tan and strong and handsome. He told me he was trying out for a few acting parts 'for when they need a wheelchair guy.' I told him I bet he would get a part that wasn't even for a wheelchair guy—just a handsome guy. He blushed when I said that. He told me he was an intern at a movie studio making cartoon drawings and models of characters and was hoping they'd keep him on after he graduates. I asked him to describe where he worked and it's exactly like the place in my Knowing, right down to the workbench that is just the right height for him and his old set of knives in the little slots on a shelf. Once he gets out of school and can work full time, he plans to get a better place for his mom and send her some money every month.

I think Ronnie was always this nice person inside, but he was mad and scared and crusted up with meanness on the outside. I think if you can help people feel safe enough around you, sometimes they can take down the shield and give you a chance to truly know them, the way I know Ronnie. After he went back to California, Ronnie got his movie role—the part of a good-looking guy who just happened to live in a wheelchair. He got a preview copy of the movie and sent it to the high school principal and suggested that the high school have a special showing to raise money for the 'Samuel and Maggie May Tindale Memorial Scholarship Fund'. How about that?

The high school rented a big projector, brought out all the chairs from the cafeteria and showed the movie outside on the wall of the gymnasium. When the whole town started showing up, they needed more chairs, so they called up all the restaurants and the owners brought theirs. CeeGee felt like she had stepped back into her Knowing when she saw Ronnie on that pier on a glorious bright California day, with the blue and white waves booming below him, just the way she had seen him in her Knowing. Everyone who came to the movie that night made donations to the scholarship fund, then helped take the chairs back to the restaurants and stayed for dinner. My family went to the Asian Pearl and sat with Elby and his parents, and Kim Soon took great care of us. Each restaurant donated the profits they made that night to the scholarship fund also, and I think some people in town chipped in extra on top of that, so it is growing.

The school is already looking for an idea for next year's fundraiser. I'm hoping Ronnie will be in another movie and send it on to us. The goal for the 'Samuel and Maggie May Tindale Memorial Scholarship Fund' is to raise enough money so that every single Southport child who wants to go to college will have the opportunity. This is what you have inspired.

Here's one more piece of news you will really like. Two years ago, a newcomer moved to the island—a woman all alone. Her name is Jessica Wilder and the first time I saw her, I felt like I knew her, like she was part of a Knowing that never quite made it to the surface. I could tell that she had a sad shadow on her past and came to the island to be safe and start over fresh. She got a job working at the marina store and soon all the fishermen in town knew Jessica. They would stop by the store to kid with her and once she got used to her new life, she brightened up and would kid them right back.

One man went out to his boat every single day for months on end, just so he had an excuse to stop by the marina store to see Jessica. Guess who that was? Our good friend Mike Robins! He finally decided that if he didn't ask her to marry him, his casket business would go to ruin. She said 'yes' and they got married in your old backyard. I helped Juan and Rosa with the reception, the way we did when the first Mrs. Robins passed on. The Robins kids have a mom at last, and they hang all over Jessica like ornaments on a Christmas tree.

Now, when I'm not babysitting for Alice and Buster's *three* kids, I'm babysitting for the Robins' *five* kids! I sit at the kitchen table with the older ones and use your old pocket knife to peel apples in a long spiral, the way you used to do for me. Sometimes I make skillet oatmeal, with a little salt, butter and raisins on top. I learned from you and my mom that if you feed kids, they will tell you anything, so I get all the news. I feel like the long story of Mike, you and me, made a big circle and Jessica is the pretty bow that came and tied it all up.

This brings me to the end of this letter and the thing I need to tell you. I won't be writing you again. Not because you aren't my friend anymore, but because I've grown up enough to know I don't have to write letters to keep you close. The same way I have learned that I don't have to have Knowings to be helpful to others. When I was little, and you left this earth, I was afraid I would lose you. I wrote letters to hang on to you. Now I know you will always be close to me, and I will never forget what you taught me because it's all part of who I am. When I look up at the night sky, I know you are there, shining bright, part of the vast beyond.

I think this is the real message of the tide pool in *Cannery Row*. Not just that we can't see everything and know everything, but that each one of us is a part of that vast unknown. When I look up at the heavens I know there are stars that I can see, and they have order and a pattern, but beyond them there is space beyond my imagination that stretches on and on. While I can neither see nor understand all of this universe, the little dot on earth that is Celia Gene Williamson is part of it. So, wherever you are, I am there as part of you and you are here as part of me. That's what I've come to believe, that all of life is connected in ways that are profound and essential and beyond our understanding.

I know one thing for sure—knowing you has shaped me. It is because of you I am the person I am today. It is the very best in me. I promise I will take all that I have learned, carry on, and make us both proud. I will help children love books and learn from them. I will follow my Guide for Giving. And if I'm lucky enough to have children of my own someday, I will teach them the five guidelines as soon as they are old enough to speak and remember. And, like Ronnie said at the marsh that day, I won't ever forget. I won't forget a single thing.

Your friend forever,
Celia Gene

Author's Notes

CeeGee's Gift began way back in the 1990's as a one act play. I was living in the small, island town of Friday Harbor, WA in the Pacific Northwest and our San Juan Island Community Theatre hosted an annual Playwrights' Festival. I had recently become ill and could no longer work. My diagnosis indicated my illness was chronic and was not likely to go away. It was a sad, difficult time and I felt useless, as if my life no longer had any value.

So, with a lot of time on my hands, I decided to write a play to enter in the festival. I remember sitting at my desk, looking out the window at Mount Baker in the distance when, surprisingly, like CeeGee's Knowings, the story came to me all at once. The characters, their names, the island setting and, most important, the message that I needed to learn in order to find meaning in my own altered life: 'The reason we are here on earth is to discover our gifts and learn how to give them. Everyone has gifts to share.'

My job, like all of us, was to discover the gifts I did have, or could develop, and give them with a generous heart. Illness did not exempt me from that purpose.

The play, twenty pages long, was entered in the Playwrights' Festival and was one of six winners. It was produced for the stage, with favorite island actors cast in each of the parts. I got to sit in a darkened theatre and see Mr. Tindale rocking on his porch. I saw the beam of light come down from above when CeeGee received a Knowing. I saw bossy Miss McGuire sashay across the stage, and sweethearts Buster and Alice and the bully, Billy Joe Jones. At the end of the three-weekend long festival, *CeeGee's Gift* received the Audience Choice Award.

I knew *CeeGee's Gift* was bigger than a 20-minute play, so after my husband and I moved to my home state of Texas, I began to expand it to a novel set on the Texas Gulf Coast where I spent my childhood vacations playing on the beach and surf fishing with my dad. While the landscape was familiar, new characters and new Knowings came into the story, as they had with the play.

I entered early manuscripts in the annual Writer's League of Texas fiction competitions. *CeeGee's Gift* was a finalist for Middle Grade Fiction in 2008 and the winner of Best Young Adult Fiction in 2010.

As the book went through draft after draft, I have been fortunate to have many volunteer readers. A high school English class, a fifth-grade class at a school for girls, a mother-daughter book club, adult book club, a group at a senior center and too many patient and caring friends to mention. My dear husband, Dan, could probably recite most of the manuscript from memory by now. I appreciate all their valuable input and because of them I consider *CeeGee's Gift* a book to be given and shared across the generations, not one written for any particular age.

As I look back on why CeeGee is the girl she is, I am reminded of qualities I had as a child, and even today. I have never been surprised by a death, nor have I ever found death tragic. If I cry at a funeral, it is not because of the loss of the person who has gone on, but rather the beauty and poetry of the remembrance.

As a child, I would sit in a restaurant or airport terminal and watch people. I knew who was arguing or sad, lonely or liberated. I could see it on them, in them. My mother told me that I was a keen observer and had a sensitive soul. As an adult, I find that people tell me their secrets. I don't know why, but perhaps it is because they sense I will not be shocked, no matter how strange the story. They sense that I somehow understand and accept the myriad complexity of life in our vast, glorious home here on earth.

I'm ready to send CeeGee out into the world now, and hope that on her journey she inspires sensitivity and kindness in others. I hope readers discover more of themselves as they come to know her and the residents of Magdalena Island, and I hope they pass on what they learn from CeeGee and Mr. Tindale.

As for me, I am ready to start a new story, in hopes there are more gifts that I can share.

☆ ☆ ☆ ☆

If you, or your Book Group, have questions about *CeeGee's Gift* or would like to participate in a discussion, please email your requests to: joy@joywrites.com.

Joy can join your group with a written response, in person or by video and would enjoy answering any questions you may have. Joy will address your comments and questions in ongoing blog posts and articles as well.

If you would like to post a review of *CeeGee's Gift*, please do so on Amazon or send to Joy to post on her website: www.JoyWrites.com.

CPSIA information can be obtained
at www.ICGtesting.com
Printed in the USA
LVHW091111110219
607073LV00002B/4/P

9 781732 283114